CORK CITY LIBRARY
Leabharlann Cathrach Chorcaí

GRA

www.corkcitylibrary.ie

Tel./Guthán (021) 4924900

This book is due for return on the last date stamped below.
Overdue fines: 10c per week plus postage.

1 3 MAR 2018

Central Adult: 4924908/9	Central Child: 4924903	Central Music: 4924919
Douglas: 4924932	Hollyhill: 4924928	Hollyhill: 4924935
St Mary's Rd Adult: 4924933	St Mary's Rd Child: 4924937	Tory Top Rd: 4924934

D1327050

TITANIC AFFAIR

Recent Titles by Amanda P. Grange

TITANIC AFFAIR

Amanda P. Grange

This first world edition published in Great Britain 2004 by
SEVERN HOUSE PUBLISHERS LTD of
9–15 High Street, Sutton, Surrey SM1 1DF.
This first world edition published in the USA 2004 by
SEVERN HOUSE PUBLISHERS INC of
595 Madison Avenue, New York, N.Y. 10022.

British Library Cataloguing in Publication Data

Grange, Amanda
    Titanic affair
    1. Titanic (Ship) - Fiction
    2. Love stories
    I. Title
    823.9'2 [F]

    ISBN 0-7278-6102-6

Typeset by Palimpsest Book Production Ltd.,
Polmont, Stirlingshire, Scotland.
Printed and bound in Great Britain by
MPG Books Ltd., Bodmin, Cornwall.

One

Miss Emilia Cavendish, kneeling in her rented room on a bright morning in the spring of 1912 with the sun gleaming on her golden hair, was packing her portmanteau in preparation for a new life with her godmother. In front of her, the portmanteau was almost full. She looked round the shabby room to make sure she had not forgotten anything, running her eyes over the iron bed, the chest of drawers and the washstand, but the surfaces were all bare. Once she had packed her last dress she would be finished.

Her thoughts returned to her coming journey and her spirits lifted. She had only to avoid Mr Montmorency for a few more hours and then she would be away from him, out of his power, and sailing on *Titanic* for her godmother's home in Ireland.

She finished her packing and was just about to close her bag when her heart skipped a beat, for she heard the sound of footsteps hurrying up the stairs.

No, he can't have found me, she thought in fright.

A moment later, she breathed a sigh of relief as Mrs Wichwood hurried into the room. However, her relief was short-lived; the kindly landlady's face was worried, and told her that something dreadful had happened.

'He's here,' said Mrs Wichwood, puffing and panting. 'Mr Montmorency. I've just seen him at the end of the street, and he's got that Mr Barker with him. He's found you.'

'Then I must go,' said Emilia, springing to her feet and fastening her portmanteau.

'Yes, dear, get away while you can. Go out the back way, then he won't see you leave.'

'Delay them as much as you can,' begged Emilia. 'Make

1

them wait at the door and then keep them talking for as long as possible.'

'Don't you fear, I'll do my best. You just worry about getting yourself down to the harbour. Good luck, my dear.'

Emilia picked up her bag, then ran down the stairs and into the kitchen.

'Write to me from Ireland,' said Mrs Wichwood, following her. 'I won't be easy in my mind until I know you've escaped.'

'I will, I promise,' said Emilia, opening the back door.

'And if he gets you before you reach the ship, you send word to me,' said Mrs Wichwood. 'I'll find a way to help you, somehow.'

'Dear Mrs Wichwood, what would I have done without you?' said Emilia gratefully. She gave the elderly woman a hug. 'Don't worry, I'll make sure they don't catch me,' she said.

Then opening the door she stepped outside. She looked left and right, trying to get her bearings as she did not often use the back door, but a moment's thought solved the problem and she turned right, heading towards the harbour. She had only to reach *Titanic* and then she would be safe.

She ran through the streets, dodging horses and carts, and weaving her way through the throng of people all heading for the quayside as they went to see the great ship set off on its maiden voyage. She turned into a side street, meaning to take a short cut . . . and saw Silas Montmorency at the other end of it. Fortunately he had not seen her. He was standing with his back to her and he was looking around him in an attitude of exasperation. He must have been to the house and discovered that he had missed her, but she reassured herself with the knowledge that he had no idea where she was going. He knew only that she had changed her lodgings again, as she had done many times over the past few weeks in a desperate bid to escape him. He had no idea she was about to leave the country.

She turned back and ran down the main street instead. The tang of salt in the air and the crying of the gulls told her that she was drawing near the harbour, and she soon found herself next to the South Western Hotel. Ahead of her was the ship. Dwarfing the White Star Line shed that stood next to it, it rose majestically from the water, and was every bit as splendid as the newspapers had claimed it to be. Its white paintwork sparkled on the upper decks and its black-topped funnels shone in the spring sunlight. But Emilia saw only one thing as she looked at it: a means of escape. If she could just cross the remaining few hundred feet she would be free.

The dock was teeming with activity. Vans were sounding their horns as they tried to deliver last-minute supplies, horses were mingling with motor cars, and everywhere there were sightseers, marvelling at the pride of the White Star Line.

Emilia slowed her pace and began to mingle with the people milling all around her. As long as she behaved just like everyone else then she would not draw attention to herself. Bit by bit, she drew closer to the ship. But just as she approached the gangplank she saw Barker, Mr Montmorency's henchman. He was not ten feet away, pushing his way through the crowd. If he looked round and saw her . . . She quickened her step and felt her spirits lighten as she reached the gangplank. Every step would help her now. She followed a beautifully dressed mother and daughter up the plank to the towering ship, and almost laughed as she reached the top and stepped on board. There was nothing either Silas Montmorency or Barker could do to her now, because even if they saw her they did not have a ticket, and without a ticket or a first class companion they would not be able to follow her. She was safe!

She began to make her way through the ship, looking about her with interest. She had never seen anything so magnificent in her life. Walking through one splendid room after another, she was amazed at how large the ship was, and thought it was more like a grand hotel. Potted palms were set in nearly every corner, graceful columns supported high ceilings, and the decorations gleamed with gold. People were everywhere. The ladies were dressed in the latest Paris fashions, with their tapering, ankle-length skirts and their knee-length coats. On their heads were set broad-brimmed hats, decorated with feathers that bobbed and swayed as they crossed the rooms or disappeared into lifts. Gentlemen in lounge suits and children in sailor suits added to the bustle. Amongst the throng hurried porters carrying luggage, and stewards seeing to the comfort and convenience of the passengers.

Emilia wove her way between the crowds until she came to a grand staircase leading upwards. It was lit from above by a huge dome, flooding the staircase with daylight and showing off the intricate carving of the banisters. Wanting to go on deck and watch the ship slip out to sea, she followed the staircase. There was a clock on the landing and she stopped to check the time. It was set into a huge arch and flanked by the carved figures of two women, and its hands showed that it was ten to twelve. She did not have long to find the deck if she wanted to see the ship set sail.

She continued upwards and emerged on deck, where a keen wind was blowing. She put a hand to her hat to make sure it didn't blow away, then she looked about her. The view was obscured by lifeboats, hanging in a row from strong davits, but in between them she could glimpse the sea. A crowd had already gathered in the gaps. To her left, people stood sedately and talked in cultured tones. To her right, further along the deck, the men in third class threw their hats in the air or lifted children on to their shoulders, whilst the women, in shabby woollen skirts and shawls, waved to people below.

Emilia turned towards the first class passengers again. She felt hesitant about joining them, but she reminded herself that she had a first-class ticket and made her way over to the rail. She had been intending to sail to Ireland later in the month, on the cheapest ship available, but then she had received her godmother's letter. An old school friend of her godmother's had had to cancel her trip on *Titanic*'s maiden voyage, and wondered if her godmother might enjoy a journey. It had been quickly arranged that Emilia should use the ticket instead, and now here she was, in the lap of luxury, with her problems about to drift away behind her.

She found a space at the railings, and leaning against it she looked down at the dock. There were hundreds of people standing there, waving handkerchiefs and calling out, 'Good luck!' There were motor vans, too, and brewers' carts, all trying to go about their business. The drivers honked their horns, but to no avail; the people on the dock were too busy cheering to notice them. She scanned the crowd, still feeling apprehensive, although she told herself there was no need, and to her relief she could see no sign of Barker or Mr Montmorency. They must have abandoned their search on the quay and gone to look for her in the town.

A whistle blew, and the atmosphere around her changed. There was a flurry of activity as those who were not intending to sail on *Titanic* began to leave the ship, anxious to make sure they did not get trapped on board. There were cries of 'Goodbye!' and 'Good luck!', then the last visitor hurried down the gangplank and set foot on dry land. The gangplanks were drawn in, the ropes were cast off, and the tugs began pulling *Titanic* out of the harbour.

There was an anxious moment when a small vessel broke its moorings and swung out towards *Titanic*. For a horrible minute Emilia thought it would crash into the ship, and that *Titanic* would have to put back into port, but one of the tugs soon managed to pull it out of the way, and then they were off, leaving Southampton behind them – Southampton, Barker and Silas Montmerency.

Emilia felt all her pent-up tension rush out of her. She was well and truly on her way. Now all she had to do was find her stateroom. The ship was so huge she had no idea where to begin, but once she hailed a passing steward, he kindly took her to the door.

'Enjoy your trip,' he said pleasantly.

'Thank you, I intend to,' she said with a smile.

She opened the door and went in. There was a splendid fireplace, a comfortable armchair and a French Empire-style table and chairs, and there were fresh flowers everywhere. How lucky she was, to be able to spend a whole day aboard!

She was just about to go into the bedroom and begin unpacking her portmanteau when there came a knock at the door. She felt a moment of apprehension. She had lived so long with fear that it would take her some time to be rid of it. But reminding herself that she had nothing to be frightened of any more, she called, 'Come in.'

The door opened, and she saw a middle-aged man standing there. He was evidently not a steward, for he was not dressed in a steward's uniform. Instead he was dressed in a smart suit, with a watch chain slung across the front of his waistcoat. He had a brisk, business-like air about him, and she had no idea what he was doing in her stateroom, as she had never seen him before in her life.

'Can I help you?' she asked, her good manners overcoming her surprise.

'It's more a question of me helping you,' he said with an ingratiating smile.

She frowned slightly. There was something about his tone she did not like. She liked him even less when, a minute later, he took a wad of bank notes out of his pocket and brandished it suggestively.

'My name is Hutton,' he said. 'I work for Mr Carl Latimer. As I'm sure you know, Mr Latimer is a very wealthy man. He's instructed me to buy your stateroom from you for the duration of the trip to America. He will give you a full refund on your ticket as well as providing you with another first-class stateroom in exchange. He is also prepared to give you fifty pounds to make amends for the inconvenience.' His smile broadened. 'This must be your lucky day.'

Emilia raised her eyebrows. 'I don't think so,' she replied. 'I'm afraid I have no intention of giving up my stateroom. Now, if there's nothing further, I will bid you good day.'

'I don't think you understand,' he said, his smile becoming fixed. 'Mr Latimer is a *very* wealthy man. He's used to getting his own way.'

'Is he?' asked Emilia coolly. 'Unfortunately, he is going to be disappointed on this occasion.'

She expected him to leave but he did not do so. Taking matters into her own hands she went over to the door, but he showed no signs of departing.

'Oh, come now, Miss Cavendish,' he said obsequiously.

'Mr Latimer will give you anything you want if you will only indulge him in this matter.' He began to peel off notes suggestively. 'What would you say to a hundred pounds?'

'I would say I'd rather you put it away,' replied Emilia curtly. 'Now, if you please, I'd like you to leave.'

'Come, come,' he said with a falsely jovial air.

'If you don't leave my stateroom at once I will call for the steward,' she said firmly.

'Two hundred,' he said.

'Not two thousand,' she replied. 'Now, are you going to leave or must I have you forcibly removed?'

His mouth became grim. 'You're making a big mistake,' he said.

Emilia opened the door wide.

He looked as though he was going to protest, but at that moment a steward hurried down the corridor. Emilia opened her mouth, preparing to call to him, but Hutton sensed defeat and stepped out of the stateroom.

'If you should change your mind . . .' he said, turning in the doorway.

'I won't,' she retorted.

Then, before he could say anything else, she shut the door behind him.

Well, she thought, as she leant back against the door, it seemed that she had escaped the clutches of one wealthy man, only to fall foul of another. Although the difference was that Mr Montmorency had wanted from her something of far more value than her stateroom.

Why was it wealthy men thought they could buy everything? she wondered. Why would they not accept that some things were simply not for sale? There was no use worrying about it, particularly when she had so many better things to do.

First of all she wanted some refreshment, and then she must find some paper and write to Mrs Wichwood. She wanted her landlady to know as soon as possible that she had escaped.

The first corridors were narrow but well lit, and she had no difficulty finding her way back to the public spaces. Once there she found a steward and asked him where she could find refreshment.

'The Café Parisien is not far from here,' he said, giving her directions.

'Thank you,' she said.

She headed towards the café, only to see the unwelcome sight of Mr Hutton heading towards her. Beside him was a gentleman with dark hair, fashionably slicked back to follow the contours of his finely-shaped head. High cheekbones and a square chin gave a decided look to his face, and there was something in his carriage which suggested he was used to command. His body was contoured with muscles that she could just see defined beneath his lounge suit. His clothes were expensive, showing evidence of London tailoring, and Emilia guessed at once who he was: Mr Carl Latimer.

At that moment he saw her. There was some talk between him and his man, and then he started walking towards her with a purposeful air – although walking was hardly the word for it; he was stalking her.

Ignoring him, she carried on her way towards the staircase, meaning to pass Mr Latimer by, but he moved to intercept her, blocking her path with his large body.

She stepped to the side.

He countered.

She stepped to the other side.

He countered again.

Then, inclining his head, he said, 'Miss Cavendish. Allow me to introduce myself. My name is Latimer. Carl Latimer.'

He smiled, and his lips parted to reveal even white teeth. Though he was dressed in fashionable and expensive clothes, there was something predatory about him, a suggestion of ruthlessness that made it easy to believe he would succeed where other men would fail. She guessed at once that his money was not inherited, but made. He had none of the ingrained poise of a gentleman born and bred, for despite his appearance of being civilized, beneath the surface there lurked something untamed. And yet for all that, she was not frightened of him, as she had been frightened of Mr Montmorency.

So, instead of trying to sidestep him again, she looked him in the eye and said coolly, 'Please stand aside.'

His smile widened, as though he appreciated her challenge. But he did not do as she asked.

'In a minute,' he said.

His voice was low and cultured, but beneath it she could detect a faint trace of a rougher accent.

'I understand you took exception to my man's visit this morning,' he went on. 'I would like to apologize for his intrusion, and for anything he said which might have upset you. It was not my intention to cause you distress, I assure you.'

His words were politeness itself, but beneath the charm was a strong will which was almost palpable.

'If you will excuse me . . .' She trailed away meaningfully, but he did not stand aside.

'Miss Cavendish, I would like to speak to you about—'

'My stateroom. I know,' she interrupted him, feeling the sooner she brought the interview to an end the better. There was something distinctly unsettling about Mr Latimer. 'But I am afraid I have no intention of relinquishing it. I intend to make use of it for my journey to Ireland as arranged.'

'Miss Cavendish,' he said, with a slight hardening of his eyes – extremely dark eyes, she noticed, the colour of rich chocolate – 'I am a very wealthy man—'

'So your man informed me,' she interrupted. 'It must be very pleasant for you, but it has nothing to do with me. Now, pray stand aside, so that I might carry on my way.'

'You're right. This is no place to be holding a conversation. I'll escort you to the library and we can discuss the matter there,' he said.

'We will do nothing of the kind. There is nothing to discuss. Now, unless you want me to call a steward I suggest you let me pass.'

He gave a slight shrug, and she expected him to move out of her way, but instead, a challenging smile crossed his face.

'Hail one,' he said.

She bit her lip. He had called her bluff, for there was not a steward in sight.

'Mr Latimer—'

'All I'm asking is that you hear me out,' he interrupted her, with a note of steel beneath the charm.

She sighed. 'Is there any other way for me to be rid of you?' she asked, her patience and her good manners exhausted.

She saw a surprised expression cross his face and then his mouth set in a straight line, as though he was not accustomed to people wanting to be rid of him – and as though he did not like the novel experience.

His smile quickly returned, but his voice had a further hardness to it when he said, 'No.'

'Very well. Now, what is it you want to say?'

'Miss Cavendish.' Now that he had won his point he hesitated, as though he wasn't sure how to continue. Then, thrusting his hands deep in his trouser pockets, he pursed his lips and went on: 'I have a sick mother . . .'

A sick mother? She was astonished. It was the last thing she had expected him to say.

'I took her to London so that I could consult the best doctors for her,' he continued, 'but I have not been able to secure the accommodation I wanted for her on her return journey. You, on the other hand, occupy one of the best staterooms on the ship. You have a sitting room as well as two bedrooms and a private deck – totally unnecessary for a healthy young woman travelling alone—'

'How do you know I am travelling alone?' she interrupted.

He waved one hand dismissively. 'I make it my business to know these things. Now, all I am asking is that you swap rooms with my mother for one night. I will recompense you handsomely and—'

'That will be quite unnecessary. I'm very sorry to hear that your mother is sick' – if you really have a sick mother, she added to herself, as she would not put it past him to invent a sick mother if it suited him – 'but my stateroom is not for sale. I mean to make use of it tonight. Tomorrow, however, once I disembark at Queenstown, it will be empty and your mother will be welcome to it.'

'I don't think you realize how wealthy I am . . .' he began, snapping his fingers in the direction of his man.

'Mr Latimer,' she said with irritation, 'I don't care. There are some things that cannot be bought.'

'Everything can be bought, for the right price,' he said, taking a cheque book from Hutton.

Emilia, seeing a steward approaching, called to him, 'Would you show me the way to the Café Parisien, please? I seem to be lost.'

'Certainly, miss. If you would care to follow me,' said the steward obligingly.

Emilia turned to Mr Latimer and said freezingly, 'I will bid you good day.'

And with that, she walked away, leaving Mr Latimer looking after her with a shrewd expression on his face.

'I'm sorry, sir,' said Hutton. 'I told you she was stubborn. If she had any sense she'd accept your offer. It's a very generous offer, if I might say so, sir.'

Carl's eyes followed her along the corridor. 'I'm glad she didn't.' His eyes kindled as he watched her recede from view. 'Life's been far too simple recently. All this easy living is making me soft. I'm in need of a challenge.' He grinned wolfishly. 'It looks like I've just found one.'

Two

'Thank you,' said Emilia to the steward as she reached the Parisien café. 'You have been most helpful.'

'Thank you, miss,' he said pleasantly.

She went into the café. It was light, airy and spacious, and had large arched windows looking out over the sea. Trellis surrounded the windows, with ivy growing through it, and white wicker furniture was set on the chequerboard floor.

She was just about to take a seat when, to her astonishment, she saw a familiar figure over by the window, sitting in a wicker chair. It was the last person she had expected to see on the ship: Freddy Longthorn.

'Freddy!' she exclaimed in surprise.

'Good Lord! Emilia!' said Freddy Longthorn, looking up from the newspaper he had been reading. 'Don't tell me you're on board? What a surprise!'

He grinned at her engagingly. Then, remembering his manners, he stood up, revealing his long gangly body dressed in flannels. He looked for all the world as though he was about to play a game of tennis.

'Are you going to play, or have you been playing?' asked Emilia humorously, as she joined him at his table.

'What? Oh, the flannels. I've been having a go in the gym, don't you know? There's a splendid fellow there, absolutely splendid, by the name of McCawley, he runs the whole show. He set me up on the horse—'

'Horse?' asked Emilia, startled.

'The electric horse,' explained Freddy. 'It's a wonderful invention. Then he set me up on the camel – electric again. It's just like riding the real thing.'

'Have you ever ridden a camel?' asked Emilia humorously.

'I can't say I have, now you come to mention it, but it's bound to be the same,' he said, laughing.

'But what are you doing on board *Titanic*?' she asked.

'Ah, well, it's a long story.'

'In that case, I had better sit down.'

He held out a chair for her and pushed it in again when she had settled herself.

'Would you like something to drink? Tea? Coffee?' he asked her.

'Yes, please. A coffee, I think.'

He ordered her a drink and then sat down opposite her. She was delighted to have met him so unexpectedly. Seeing him took her back to the happy days of her childhood, when her parents had been alive. Freddy had lived in the largest house in the village of Chipping Burton, whilst her family had occupied a neat house nearby. She and Freddy had been the same age, and when they had been babies their nursemaids had taken them to the park together to feed the ducks. As they had grown older they had spent much of their time playing together, to say nothing of trying to avoid Freddy's forceful nurse, Hildegarde. Those times, alas, had ended on her parents' death, when she had moved away from the neighbourhood, but they still brought back happy memories.

'The thing is . . .' said Freddy.

'Yes?' said Emilia, encouragingly.

He looked suddenly sheepish.

'The thing is . . .'

'You're in some kind of trouble,' she said. 'What is it this time? Have you been sent to America by your father in order to learn a trade, or have you been banished on account of a worse-than-usual prank?'

'Good Lord, no, whatever makes you think that?' he asked. 'No, no, it's nothing like that.' His tone changed. 'It's worse.'

'Then you had better tell me all about it,' said Emilia.

The waiter brought over two cups of coffee. Once he had left, Freddy said, 'You're taking it very lightly, but you won't when you know what the trouble is. The thing is, Emilia, I'm engaged.'

'Engaged?' Emilia was surprised. 'To be married?'

'That's the usual sort of engagement,' he said testily.

'In that case, congratulations.'

'Yes, well, no . . . the thing is,' he confided, 'that's why I'm going to Cherbourg.'

'Then you're not going to New York?'

'No. Cherbourg's the place for me.'

'Is your fiancée French?' asked Emilia, having difficulty in following Freddy's conversation.

'No she isn't. Quite the opposite, as a matter of fact. She's as English as they come. Her name is Ellison. Penelope Ellison.'

'Then why are you going to France?' asked Emilia, mystified.

'Can't stand the French,' said Freddy. 'Penelope, that is. She calls them a nation of snail eaters. She won't set foot in the place.'

'Ah.' Emilia's mouth quirked. 'I see. The engagement, I take it, is not to your liking?'

'No, it isn't,' he admitted.

'Then why did you propose?' asked Emilia reasonably.

'I didn't,' he said mournfully. 'She proposed to me. Or rather, she said, "Freddy, I've decided to marry you". Then she dragged me into the ballroom and said, "Everyone, Freddy and I are engaged".'

'Oh, dear,' said Emilia, unable to suppress a smile.

'It's all very well for you. You're not engaged to a harridan with a dozen brothers and a father who's a crack shot.'

'They all hate France?' queried Emilia.

'Every last one of 'em,' said Freddy.

'Now I see why you're going there! Well, if they all hate it, you should be safe.'

'Ah! France. La belle France,' said Freddy with a sigh, relaxing back into his wicker chair. 'Moulin Rouge . . . croissants . . . Burgundy . . . Brie . . . In a few hours' time I'll be safe from Penelope and her whole benighted family.'

'How long are you going for?' asked Emilia.

'For as long as it takes.'

'As long as it takes for what?' she asked, startled.

'For her to find some other poor chap to get engaged to. I don't fancy the curate's chances. He's a weak-looking fellow, with no backbone,' he said, pursing his lips.

'Would Penelope want to marry a curate?' she asked curiously.

'I don't see why not. Her uncle's a clergyman. It runs in the family. Anyway, he's available and I'm not.'

He gave a sigh of satisfaction. 'This is the life, Emilia. It's a pity I'm not on board longer. But how about you? What are you doing going to America?'

'I'm not going to America. I'm going to Ireland,' said Emilia. 'I'm going to live with my godmother.'

'Really? Good for you. But what about your Aunt Clem?'

Emilia's smile faded. 'She died.'

'Oh, I say, Emilia, I'm sorry,' said Freddy.

'Yes, so am I.'

'But you'll enjoy living with your godmother,' said Freddy bracingly.

'Yes, you're right. I'm looking forward to it.'

'It's a pity you're not going to New York. You could have looked in on Charlie. He's got a job out there.'

Emilia's eyes widened. 'Charlie Potter? A job?'

Charlie had also lived in Chipping Burton, and had been a great friend of Freddy's. He was a small, round person and in his childhood he had had a love of jam tarts and practical jokes.

'I can't blame you for being surprised, but it's true. Here.' He took a card out of his pocket and handed it to her: CHARLIE POTTER, EXPERT ON FINE ANTIQUES. It was followed by a smart address in New York.

'Does Charlie know anything about antiques?' she asked in surprise.

'Oh, Lord, yes. Well, no . . . no, not really, but he's doing very well out there.'

'What made him think of selling antiques in New York?'

'You might well ask. It's all on account of Julia.'

'Julia?'

'Yes. Charlie's in love again.'

'Ah, I see.'

Charlie fell in and out of love with alarming regularity, but he had never before, to Emilia's knowledge, carried things so far as to take up employment.

'I assume he wants to impress Julia's father?' she asked.

'Got it in one. He asked for her hand. He was turned down, of course – her father couldn't give his daughter to a man with no means of support, he said. He wouldn't take the trust fund as means. Nothing but honest labour. So off Charlie went to America and somehow fell into antiques. It was all on account of his being English. It made people think he knew what he was talking about. They don't have them over there, apparently – antiques, that is, not English people. The country's not old enough. He got himself employed by a firm that liked the sound of his voice and is doing jolly well, apparently.'

'Good for him!' smiled Emilia. 'Will you be on board for dinner?' she asked, when she and Freddy had finally caught up with all their news.

Freddy shook his head. 'No. Unfortunately not. *Titanic* docks about half past five. I'll be in France for dinner. A nice cutlet and a bottle of wine.'

'Would you like to look round the rest of the ship with me whilst you're still aboard?' she asked.

Freddy shook his head. 'No, thanks all the same. I've seen it. I boarded early. Promised old McCawley I'd go back and give his camel another go. I wouldn't mind a look round your stateroom, though. I haven't had a chance to see one. They're very grand by all accounts, though I can't see why they call them staterooms. They seem more like suites to me.'

'They are,' said Emilia. 'Mine is wonderful. Come and see it when you've finished in the gym. Shall we say, half past three? I can arrange for the stewardess to bring us tea.'

'Rightio,' said Freddy.

'Do you know where I'll find any writing paper?' asked

Emilia, as they were about to part. 'I promised to write a letter to a friend.'

'In the reading room,' said Freddy promptly. 'It's very smart. It's headed with the white star flag, and says: On board R.M.S. *TITANIC*. I wrote a letter to the mater. I thought it would please her.'

'I'm sure it will. Can I post it on board?'

He pursed his lips. 'I don't know. I gave mine to my man. Ask a steward, he'll be bound to know.'

Thanking Freddy for his advice, Emilia decided to go back to her room first for a shawl. The ship was heated but her dress was thin and she was feeling rather cold. Once she had fetched it she would go to the reading room and then write her letter to Mrs Wichwood.

Carl Latimer was standing in the sitting room of his mother's stateroom with a frown on his face. He had hoped the trip to Europe would be beneficial to her, and that the London doctors would be able to tell him what was wrong with her, but, like the New York doctors, their diagnoses had been vague.

'A nervous indisposition' had been the general consensus of opinion, but it told him nothing. His mother had never been a nervous woman, indeed she had been extremely robust in her prime. But ever since his father had died she had gradually dwindled into a hesitant woman with very little energy, a shadow of her former self.

He had done everything he could to make life easier for her after the blow of his father's death, but instead of making her better it had only seemed to make matters worse. At last he had taken to consulting doctors, the best men in their field. They had shaken their heads and looked grave; talked about tonics and rest, but none of them had seemed to be able to cure her.

The trip to Europe had been his last hope. But again the diagnoses had been vague. So now he was taking her back to New York, with another doctor in tow.

He had decided, at first, to rely on the ship's doctors for the voyage, but his mother had been so nervous that he had decided to engage Dr Allerton, to accompany her on the trip. The good doctor was with her now, checking that the vessel's departure hadn't unduly unsettled her.

The door of the bedroom opened and Dr Allerton came out. He was a small man with a grave manner, dressed in sober style, with the customary doctor's black bag.

'How is she?' asked Carl.

The doctor shook his head. 'Her nerves are disordered. She must have complete rest. I have given her companion a bottle of tonic to administer to Mrs Latimer before each meal. I rely on you to see that she takes it.'

'You can be sure I will. Is there nothing else that can be done for her?'

'No, I'm afraid not. It's a question of complete rest. Keep her quiet. Don't allow her to exert herself, and all will be well.'

Carl looked towards the door of the bedroom. His mother came out, leaning on the arm of her companion. She was not a small woman, but she seemed to have shrunk in recent years. Her complexion had dimmed, and her hazel eyes had become sunken. She was too thin. Her high-waisted Empire gown was tied with a sash which accentuated the narrowness of her frame. Not even its expensive cut could disguise the fact that her arms and shoulders were bony.

He went forward and kissed her on the cheek. 'How are you feeling?' he asked.

'A little better, I think,' she said with a weak smile.

'Good.' His voice was hearty, but he was moved to pity as he looked at her. She had lost her sparkle, and her joy in life.

He must make a more determined effort to persuade Miss Cavendish to relinquish her stateroom, he thought. It was not that his mother's room was small. Far from it. Although he had booked the rooms at short notice, he had had plenty of choice. Uncertain if the ship would sail because of the coal strike that had plagued England recently, a number of people had decided to delay their travel plans, with the result that *Titanic* was only two thirds full. But he had not been able to engage one of the promenade suites for his mother. Though she kept voicing a wish for some fresh air, the doctors expressly forbade it, but at least a private, covered promenade deck would give her an opportunity to take some exercise if she wished, without exposing her to the April chill.

Miss Cavendish would have to give in to him sooner or later. He would just have to make sure it was sooner.

Emilia left the Café Parisien behind her and made her way to her stateroom in search of her shawl. As she went along the corridor she passed one of the other first-class staterooms and stopped, arrested by the sound of a weak voice, which held a wistful tone.

'If I could just have a breath of air . . . I'm sure I would feel so much better if I could only go outside.'

'My dear lady,' came the soothing rejoinder, 'it would be most unwise. The air is cold and the wind is biting. Going outside would be most injurious to your health.'

'Oh, yes, *most* injurious,' twittered a female voice. 'Far better to stay in your stateroom where it is nice and warm.'

Emilia felt a moment of sympathy for the elderly lady, whom she could just glimpse through the open door. Her brown hair was pinned back into a severe chignon, and her skin looked grey. Her eyes were dull, and her shoulders drooped.

How dreadful for her to be cooped up inside when she longed for fresh air. But her attendant must know what was best for her, Emilia reflected, and passed on down the corridor.

She returned to her stateroom, where she picked up her shawl and draped it over her empire-line dress. With its long skirt and its long sleeves, her dress was one of the few fashionable things she possessed. It displayed the new empire line, with a high waist, a narrow skirt and a square neck. She had made it herself, out of an orientally-inspired piece of material which she had found in a sale, and although she was not particularly gifted with a needle the result had been surprisingly good.

She went back along the corridor. As she passed the door of the stateroom she had previously noticed, a man came out.

He was short and wiry, dressed in sober clothes, and he was carrying a doctor's bag. He must be the physician who attended the elderly lady, thought Emilia, and whose voice she had heard earlier.

'Is the lady terribly ill?' she asked on an impulse.

'Ill?' He looked startled, then gave a grin. 'No, of course she's not ill. There's nothing wrong with her. These old cats are all the same. They want to be told how poorly they are so they don't have to do a shred of work, and can cosset and coddle themselves all day long. If you take my advice,' he went on, looking Emilia up and down and evidently not fooled by her fashionable dress, 'you'll ingratiate yourself with the companion and get her to introduce you to the old lady. She's as rich as Croesus, and a pretty young thing like you could wangle a good deal of money out of her one way and another. It's a shame to see you in that home-made dress, when there's a lot of ugly old women on board turned out in the best style.'

Emilia, whose surprise had begun to turn to anger during the course of this speech, was outraged. 'Well, really,' she said.

She didn't know whether to be most annoyed because the doctor was misleading his patient, or because he thought she was the type of young woman to ingratiate herself with a wealthy woman in the hope of a reward.

The doctor laughed. 'You've got to get what you can in this world,' he said. 'You might as well wake up to that fact. Once you do, you won't have to wear home-made dresses any more. You just think about what I've said.'

Then, tipping his hat, he went on his way.

Of all the mercenary charlatans! exclaimed Emilia to herself. I've a good mind to go in there and tell that lady she's being exploited, she thought.

And then, before she could think better of it, she gave way to the impulse, and opened the door of the stateroom and went in.

'I'm so sorry to disturb you,' she said, 'but I feel I must speak to you—'

She broke off. For there, standing in the middle of the room,

20

was not the elderly lady she had seen earlier, but Mr Carl Latimer!

She looked at him in amazement, and then felt herself start to colour as he looked at her in astonishment.

She did not wonder at it. Whatever must he think of her? But she couldn't see how it had happened. This was definitely the room the old lady's voice had been coming from, so what was Mr Latimer doing here?

And then his words came back to her. *My mother is sick,* he had said. She had not believed him, but now to her chagrin she realized that he had been speaking the truth.

'I'd hoped you'd give better game,' he said under his breath, when he had evidently recovered from his surprise. Then, louder, he went on: 'But I suppose I should be pleased, for my mother's sake, if not my own.'

Emilia did not know what to make of this speech.

'I knew you'd come to your senses. It was just a matter of time,' he continued.

She coloured even more deeply, as she realized he thought she had come to sell him her room.

'I have done nothing of the kind,' she returned. 'That is, I was never out of my senses. That is not why I am here.'

'No?' he asked her disbelievingly. 'You make a habit of bursting into other people's rooms for no particular reason? Come now, Miss Cavendish, admit it. You have seen the sense in accepting my offer and you are here to talk terms.'

'I am here to do nothing of the sort,' she retorted. 'I am determined to keep my stateroom. My godmother would be most disappointed if I did not.'

'Then why are you here?' he asked her.

She was about to blurt it out when she suddenly thought better. She had entered the stateroom on impulse, intent on telling the elderly lady that her doctor was a charlatan and that there was no reason why she could not take a stroll on deck if she wanted to, but now it seemed an impertinence. In fact, it seemed uncomfortably like interference. Nevertheless, she had to say something if she was to wipe the infuriatingly mocking smile from Mr Latimer's lips, and the truth was her

21

best option. She took a deep breath, flexing her hands unconsciously by her side, then said, 'I came to tell your mother that her doctor is a fraud.'

He looked startled. Then his eyes narrowed. 'Did you indeed? That is a most interesting statement. You have good reason, I suppose, for blackening the good doctor's character?'

She flushed again, but she had to go on. 'I do. As I passed this room earlier, I heard your mother saying she would like some fresh air. I also heard her doctor telling her she must not have any—'

'Quite right.' He spoke quietly, but there was a hard edge to his voice. 'My mother's health is precarious. The April weather would be positively dangerous to her.'

'No. It wouldn't.'

She saw his brow darken and bit her lip. She was getting drawn into an argument about something that was none of her business, and a part of her felt she should apologize and leave the room immediately. But the wistful note she had heard in Mrs Latimer's voice compelled her to continue.

'I bumped into the doctor coming out of your mother's room,' she went on. 'He told me there was nothing wrong with your mother, that she was nothing more than a rich old woman who wanted to be pampered . . .'

She trailed off as she saw his face darken still further. His eyebrows had drawn down over his eyes, which were lit by an angry gleam, and his mouth was grim.

'I don't know what you hope to gain by this tale,' he said, 'but it won't work. Dr Allerton has put himself to considerable inconvenience in order to accompany my mother on this trip, and by so doing he has proved himself devoted to my mother's care. He is a respected doctor, one of the best in his field, and comes highly recommended.'

'Nevertheless, he is a charlatan—'

'Who just happened to tell you so himself?' he asked scathingly. 'Now tell me, Miss Cavendish, why would he do something like that?'

'Because . . .' She clenched her hands. She wanted to stop,

but her honesty had been called into question and she found she could not. She took a deep breath. 'Because he saw my home-made gown, and taking me to be as mercenary as himself he suggested I ingratiate myself with your mother in the hope of gaining a reward.'

His expression changed, and she suspected he had not believed a single word.

'Enough of this,' he said. 'My offer to pay you handsomely for your stateroom still stands, but unless you are prepared to relinquish it to me, then we have nothing further to say to each other.'

'As to that, you have already had my answer,' she said with dignity.

'Then I mustn't keep you,' he said.

Emilia turned to leave the room, but then made a last attempt to brighten Mrs Latimer's life. 'Won't you at least get a second opinion?'

'I have had not only a second, but a third, opinion,' he said coldly. 'My mother has had the most expensive doctors, both here and in America.'

And that was what probably lay at the heart of the problem, she thought. There was a fortune to be made in convincing Mrs Latimer that she was ill and in need of constant medical attention.

'The most expensive are not always the best,' she ventured.

'I believe you were leaving,' he remarked.

Emilia hesitated, then realizing she could do no more, she swept out of the room.

The whole incident had shaken her. Mrs Latimer had seemed a dear, and she had longed to help her, but Mrs Latimer's son was another matter. Not even his striking face could disguise the fact that he was ruthless and cynical.

Although he wasn't entirely ruthless, she was forced to amend her thoughts. He cared for his mother, and was doing his best to provide her with proper care. It was just that his wealth blinded him to what she really needed. She did not need cosseting, she needed stimulation. If she was not really ill, then being forced to behave as an invalid must be very tiring for her, not to mention depressing to her spirits. And if she was not used to a life of idleness – if, as Emilia suspected, Mr Latimer was a self-made man, and his mother had at one stage in her life been poor and therefore very busy – it must be even worse.

Still, there was nothing she could do about it, and she must endeavour to put it out of her mind.

Carl felt himself seething as the door closed behind Miss Cavendish. Try as he might to ignore what she had said he found he could not forget it, and even worse, he could not help wondering whether she'd been right. Ever since rising from the most crushing poverty he had put his faith in money and what money could do, but he wasn't a fool. He knew that frauds existed – he'd sent enough about their business in his time – and he knew they preyed on the wealthy. Which left him with the question, were the physicians he had consulted capable doctors, who had correctly diagnosed a nervous disorder and sensibly prescribed his mother warmth and quiet? Or were they quacks, who were keen to make as much money as they could out of him by pretending that his mother was ill when she was perfectly well?

He crossed to the porthole, looking out over the ocean.

It was a strange thing for Miss Cavendish to have said if it wasn't true. But then, what did he know about Miss Cavendish, beyond the fact she had the clearest blue eyes he had ever seen?

Now where had that thought come from? he asked himself. Miss Cavendish's eyes were not of the slightest interest to him . . . even if they were an unusual shade of blue – almost sapphire, making a stunning complement to her golden hair.

But this was nonsense. Miss Cavendish wasn't an eligible young lady to be admired, she was a thorn in his side. How had she managed to unsettle him? he wondered. By challenging him? Yes. But not in the way he'd imagined. He'd thought she would challenge him on ground he was sure of, making him exert himself to the utmost in order to persuade her to relinquish her stateroom. Instead, she'd challenged him on ground he was much less sure of, awakening doubts over his mother's illness and the doctors he employed.

Fortunately, it would not be long before she was off the ship, and then he would be able to take over her stateroom. He was uncomfortably aware, however, that he would not be able to take it over any earlier. For the first time in many years, in either personal matters or business matters, he had to acknowledge that he had been defeated.

Unaware of the disturbance she had caused Mr Latimer, Emilia retired to the reading room where she found plenty of headed note paper, and wrote to Mrs Wichwood, then returned to her stateroom in time to meet Freddy for tea.

'I say, Emilia, you've fallen on your feet,' said Freddy as he looked round her suite with admiration, going from the sitting room to the two bedrooms, and then out on to the covered deck.

The room was decorated in Tudor style, with black-and-white walls, but there its resemblance to the sixteenth century ended. It was furnished with the most up-to-the-minute wicker furniture and was decorated with potted palms. It exuded a feeling of airiness and spaciousness, and was made even more cheerful by the sunlight falling through the windows and dappling the floor, for although it was only April, the day was remarkably fine.

'Do you like it?' she asked.

'Rather.'

After asking her stewardess to bring them some tea, Emilia settled herself in one of the reclining deckchairs. Freddy took a chair next to her, and they both enjoyed the sunshine and the splendid view over the ocean.

'A life on the ocean wave, eh?' he said, sighing with contentment and stretching out on his deckchair.

Mrs McLaren entered with the tray of tea, which she put down on a nearby console table.

'Steward service, too,' said Freddy appreciatively. 'Or, rather, stewardess service. Just what you need!'

Emilia poured two cups of tea and handed one to Freddy.

'I say,' he said, sitting up and taking it. 'I couldn't help noticing you coming out of Latimer's room earlier on. It's none of my business, of course, but ought you to be getting thick with millionaires?'

'How . . . . ?'

'I was trying to find Smithers – you remember Smithers, my valet?'

'I do,' said Emilia, pleased that the capable Smithers was accompanying Freddy on his flight from Penelope.

'Well, I was trying to find him. I happened to look down one of the corridors and I saw you by Latimer's room. I met Latimer in London,' he explained. 'He introduced himself. He wanted to get into the club. He's a fine chap, but I didn't think he'd be your type.'

'He isn't,' said Emilia.

'Good. He's a bit of a ruthless chap. They're all the same, these millionaires. Give him a wide berth, that's my advice.'

'Thank you, Freddy. I intend to,' she said.

They finished their tea, catching up on all the rest of their news, before Freddy decided it was time to gather his things together in preparation for leaving the ship. Due to the incident at Southampton when the smaller vessel had snapped its moorings, *Titanic* was almost an hour late in reaching France, but at half past six, just as the sun was setting, the ship arrived.

'*La belle France*,' said Freddy, as he picked up his portmanteau, whilst his valet materialized out of nowhere, carrying a large suitcase. 'Ah! There you are, Smithers. Good show.'

The three of them waited with the other passengers who were disembarking whilst the gangplank was let down. As *Titanic* was so large, she could not get too close to shore, so a tender came out in order to take the passengers ashore. But once the gangplank had been let down, it swayed alarmingly. There was a strong wind, and it took ten men on either side to hold it down.

Freddy coughed nervously. 'I don't like the look of that,' he said.

'I'm sure it will be all right,' said Emilia reassuringly.

Smithers added murmurs of encouragement, and at last Freddy plucked up the courage to leave the ship.

'Goodbye, Emilia. Take care.'

Emilia waved him off, watching until he was lost to view, then began to take an interest in all the other things that were going on. The stop at Cherbourg was a busy one, with passengers disembarking and new passengers coming on board. Emilia recognized a number of them from the newspapers. There was millionaire Benjamin Guggenheim – she overheard him remarking to a companion that he had originally booked passage on *Lusitania*, but that he had transferred to *Titanic* when *Lusitania* had been laid up for repairs. There was a formidable-looking woman, who was addressed as Mrs Brown, and there was Lady Duff-Gordon with her husband Sir Cosmo, as well as a number of second class passengers and what seemed like a hundred passengers for steerage.

She felt a slight qualm at the thought of mixing with so many fashionable people when her own clothes were so shabby, but she did not mean to let it affect her enjoyment. If she had to go in to dinner in her home-made gown and endure the stares of the other diners, so be it.

With this resolve in mind, she headed towards the dining room, little knowing how soon it was to be tested. As she came to the seating area outside the dining room she heard the sound of smothered laughter and a woman's voice saying, 'My dear, have you ever seen anything like it? Look over there! Do you see the girl in the home-made dress! She must have wandered in from steerage. Do you think I should tell the stewards?'

'No, don't,' came another woman's voice. 'It is too delicious. I only hope she goes into the dining room. I am longing to see if she knows which cutlery to use.'

'She's probably more used to eating with her fingers, don't you think, Carl?' came the first voice.

Emilia flushed. It was bad enough to be humiliated, but to be humiliated in front of Mr Latimer seemed somehow worse.

'Oh, I don't know,' he replied. 'She probably knows how to use a fork and spoon, but I doubt if anyone knows how to use a knife as efficiently as you do, Ida.'

There was a stunned silence from the ladies. Emilia's mouth

quirked, and looking up she caught Carl Latimer's eye in one of the gilded mirrors. He inclined his head, and she inclined hers in reply. He had been bested in the matter of her stateroom, and she had been routed when trying to help his mother, but it seemed an uneasy truce had been declared between them. She only hoped it would last until she disembarked in just over twelve hours' time.

Three

'There are ten floors on the *Titanic*, miss,' said the waiter helpfully as Emilia studied the breakfast menu the following morning. 'There are the state rooms, of course, then there are the sitting rooms, libraries, cafés, Turkish baths and the exercise rooms. The gymnasium is just off the boat deck, and the swimming pool—'

'Swimming pool?' asked Emilia in surprise.

'Yes, miss. It might not be filled yet. The water's too dirty close to shore and we have to wait until we're in the open sea, but it will soon be ready for use. Then there's the squash court, and of course it's very pleasant up on deck.'

'I won't have time to see half of it, or even a quarter,' said Emilia. 'I'll be leaving the ship at Queenstown. We dock at lunchtime, I think?'

'Yes, miss, that's right.'

'I will just have to see how much I can fit in before then.'

She had managed to see the reading room, the library, the gymnasium and the dining room the night before, where not even the titters of some of the ladies at the sight of her home-made dress had been able to dim her enjoyment, but there was still plenty more for her to see.

After a wonderful breakfast of fresh fruit, poached eggs, and soda and sultana scones with Norborne honey and Oxford marmalade, she carried on with her explorations, but as she was about to climb the Grand Staircase she saw a familiar figure. It was the elderly lady she had glimpsed through the door the day before, Mrs Latimer, and she was sitting on the bottom step, looking most unwell.

29

Emilia went over to her in concern. 'Are you feeling all right?' she asked.

'No, dear, I'm feeling a bit queer,' said Mrs Latimer in a weak voice. 'Can you help me up, do you think? It's my legs. They won't do what I want them to.'

Emilia felt a rush of guilt. She had told Mr Latimer there was nothing wrong with his mother, and had suggested the elderly lady be encouraged to go on deck, but she had been quite wrong. She only hoped it was not her own words that had caused the present situation. If Mrs Latimer had heard her talking the day before, and then been encouraged to go out alone with such disastrous results, Emilia felt she would never forgive herself.

Why had she interfered? she asked herself in mortification, as she put her hand gently beneath Mrs Latimer's elbow. 'Is your companion not with you?' she said, as Mrs Latimer, half-risen, fell back on to the stair again.

'No, dear. She's feeling poorly so I left her behind. She doesn't travel well. It's the throbbing of the engines. They make her feel sick.'

Emilia felt worse and worse. Still, it was useless to indulge in self-recrimination. She must do what she could to help Mrs Latimer, and to make sure the elderly lady returned safely to her room.

'Thank you,' said Mrs Latimer, as she finally managed to rise to her feet with Emilia's help. 'You're a good girl.'

'It's the least . . .' began Emilia, only to be arrested by the sound of a strong masculine voice behind her.

'What the devil do you think you are doing?'

Emilia turned round with a sinking feeling to see Carl Latimer striding towards her, glaring ferociously. His dark eyes were smouldering, and his mouth was set in a grim line.

'I am trying to help—' she began.

'Help?' he demanded as he almost drew level with her. 'Inducing my mother to leave the safety of her stateroom and take a walk about the ship, without even so much as her companion to assist her? And that is what you call helping?'

'I didn't—' began Emilia, her sense of injustice starting to rise with this false accusation.

'And with what result? She collapses on the stairs.'

He put his arm solicitously around his mother's shoulder as she staggered, and helped her to keep her feet.

'I suggest you refrain from any further meddling in other people's affairs,' he said over his shoulder as he escorted his mother away from the stairs and towards her room.

Emilia was tempted to make an angry retort, but his words so exactly matched her own feelings that the words died on her tongue. She should have refrained from meddling. She had done no good. On the contrary, she had done a great deal of harm. Making matters worse was the fact that a number of curious glances were being directed towards her. Feeling distinctly uncomfortable, Emilia turned to go towards the deck.

'Got a mighty fine suitor there,' said a formidable woman, dressed in grand style. She had the appearance of a very wealthy woman, but a twang in her voice suggested she had not always been wealthy. Emilia recognized her as Mrs Brown, the Denver millionairess who had joined the ship at Cherbourg.

'Suitor?' she said, shaking her head. 'He is not my suitor. He can hardly bear to look at me.'

'Is that so? Seems to me a man doesn't cut up so rough about his mother unless his feelings are involved.'

'You don't understand,' said Emilia. 'She's been very ill.'

Mrs Brown nodded. 'I know all about it. I've met Carl a time or two in America.' She looked at Emilia appraisingly. 'How long are you staying on board?'

'Until Queenstown,' said Emilia.

'Pity. If you were on board until New York we might see some fireworks. It would set a few of the old biddies here by their heels, that's for sure.'

'I don't understand,' said Emilia, perplexed.

'No. I don't think you do,' laughed Mrs Brown. 'Enjoy the rest of your trip, my dear, and don't worry about Mrs Latimer. She'll pull through.'

'What a lot of fuss,' said Mrs Latimer as her son steered her gently along the corridor, back towards her room.

'I find you collapsed on the staircase and take you back to

your room and you call it a fuss? You forget how weak you are. You shouldn't be out of bed.'

She sighed, and stopped, shaking off his arm. 'Oh, yes, I should. I've been thinking about it for a while now. I've tried telling you once or twice, but you were always saying the doctors were right. I knew a breath of fresh air would cheer me up, but they made such a fuss about it I got frightened and gave in.'

'They were right. Look what happened as soon as you left your room. You'd hardly gone any distance before you collapsed,' he reminded her sternly.

'Now what's distance got to do with anything? I hadn't found my sea legs, that's all. This *Titanic*'s a marvel, but it's still a ship and I lost my balance.'

'But the doctor—'

'The doctor's a cheat. I heard that girl talking to you yesterday, and a good thing I did. It made my spirits rise, I can tell you!'

He looked uncertain.

'Now then, Carl, don't you believe me?'

He pursed his lips. 'Every doctor we've ever had—'

'Have a look at me,' she said. 'Do I look poorly?'

He scanned her face, then gave a rueful smile. Her eyes were sparkling with unwonted vitality, her complexion looked fresh and vibrant, and there was an animation to her features that hadn't seen there for a very long time indeed.

'I have to say I can't remember having seen you look so well for years.'

'That's more like it. You're a good boy, Carl, but if you try and put me back in that sickroom we'll have words. I shouldn't have gone into it in the first place, or any other sickroom either, for that matter, but there's no use crying over spilled milk. I'm alive again now, and that's the way I'm going to stay.'

'You don't just look alive, you look young,' he told her truthfully.

'Well, so I should,' she replied. 'I was only eighteen when I had you. I'm not even fifty yet, you know.'

He looked surprised.

'You'd forgotten. So had I, until that girl reminded me that I wasn't an old lady. And now you've frightened her off,' she said with a glint in her eye.

He laughed.

'What's so funny?' she asked.

'You are,' he said with a smile. 'You sound exactly as you used to, before you took to your bed. Before . . .'

'Before your father died?'

He nodded.

Her face fell. 'It was a bad time, and that's the truth, but what's done is done. I've got to make the best of it, and I've got that young woman to thank for making me see it. If she hadn't come in, I'd still be in that sickroom. Would you believe it, I was so used to being treated like an invalid I'd started thinking I must be one. You'd better go and find her, Carl, and ask her to have her dinner with us.'

He pursed his lips. 'I can't do that, I'm afraid. She's leaving the ship at Queenstown.'

His mother looked surprised. 'How do you know that?' she asked. 'I didn't know you knew her.'

'I don't. But I tried to buy her stateroom from her and she told me I could have it when she left the ship. She'll be disembarking at midday.'

'Well! So she got the better of you, did she? I like her more and more,' she said with a twinkle in her eye. 'You'd better go find her straightaway then. You can tell her you're sorry for speaking to her like that, and I can say thank you to her before she gets off the ship.'

He put his hands in his pockets. Although he saw the sense of his mother's suggestion, he wasn't looking forward to speaking to Miss Cavendish. He was going to have to eat humble pie, and it wasn't a dish he liked. But Miss Cavendish had helped his mother; he owed her for that. And whatever else he might or might not be, Carl Latimer was a man who paid his debts.

Emilia made an effort to put Mrs Latimer and the infuriating

Mr Latimer out of her mind as she explored the ship. There was so much to see that she soon became engrossed as she wandered between decks, investigating as many rooms as she could before it was time for her to disembark. She was amazed to see that the accommodation in second class was almost as good as that in first class, for although the carving on the woodwork was less ornate, it was still sumptuous. The dining saloon was panelled in oak, and the library was panelled in sycamore. There were bars in which the passengers could while away their time, and a barber's shop selling pennants and postcards and other souvenirs of the voyage. She bought a postcard for her godmother, with a picture of *Titanic* on the front. It had the White Star emblem in the top left-hand corner, and the ship's name across the top. She decided she would post it on board. It was probably the only opportunity she would ever have of sending a postcard from a ship.

She caught a glimpse of several cabins through open doorways, and although they were not as large as those in first class, they were still spacious and well appointed, with basins for washing and mahogany furniture.

She wandered on, storing everything away in her memory to tell her godmother, until she realized that her surroundings were becoming less sumptuous. She had descended several flights of stairs in search of the swimming pool, but there was no sign of it, and with a feeling of dismay she realized that she was lost.

By the look of the cabins she saw through a few open doors, she guessed she had wandered into third class, for the cabins were smaller, and bunks were provided instead of beds. She passed through a large communal room, panelled in pine, where people were talking and passing the time. Instead of comfortable chairs interspersed with potted plants as there were in first class, there were only wooden benches, whilst exposed pipework hung from the ceiling. Instead of ornate light fittings, there were bare light bulbs protected by wire cages, but still it was clean and fresh.

There were a number of people talking or playing cards. Over in the corner a group of women, some wearing plain skirts and blouses, and others wearing dark coloured dresses over which they wore woollen shawls, were talking animatedly about the new life they hoped to find in America. Nearby, a group of men, coatless, with their sleeves rolled up and their braces stretched tightly over their rough shirts, were playing dominoes. Between the benches ran children, the girls in dresses with white aprons and the boys in knee length trousers with rough jackets, enjoying the relative freedom of the room after the confines of the cabins.

Emilia decided to ask for directions. She doubted if any of the passengers in steerage knew the way to first class, but if they could direct her to the deck, she could then walk along it until she came to the first-class section, and from there she could find her way back to her stateroom.

She found the women friendly and they soon told her the way. Thanking them, she set off towards the staircase. However, just as she turned a corner and came in sight of the staircase she stopped suddenly and shrank back against the wall, her heart hammering in her chest. There, standing at the foot of the steps, was a man she recognized. A man she dreaded. He was short and stocky, with cropped blond hair and sloping shoulders, dressed in workman's clothes. It was Silas Montmorency's henchman, Barker.

What was Barker doing on board *Titanic*? she wondered. He must have seen her get on board, and followed her. But how? He didn't have a ticket, and he would not have had time to buy one. She had boarded the ship with only ten minutes to spare.

Her mind returned to more pressing concerns. She could go no further. If she continued on her way towards the stairs he would see her and it would all be over with her. It had been difficult enough getting away from him in England. The last thing she wanted was to have him follow her to Ireland.

She began to back away. She had almost managed to slip round the corner, out of sight, when he turned round. She froze again, hoping the shadows would hide her, but it was no good. His eyebrows shot up, then his mouth curved into a crooked smile. He had seen her.

Their eyes locked for a tense minute, and then she turned and ran, neither knowing or caring where she was going, driven only by a need to get away from him. She knew without looking that he was following her, for she could hear the steel caps on his shoes tapping on the floor as he ran after her. If she could just get away from him, then lose him in the labyrinthine passages of the ship, she might have a chance of escape. She had only to return to her stateroom and collect her luggage and then she could disembark. The ship would be docking at Queenstown in less than an hour. As long as he did not see her, the ship would be heading for New York before he realized she was no longer on it.

She threaded her way through the third-class passengers, past gossiping women and men playing fiddles, avoiding children's hoops and balls, every few minutes glancing over her shoulder to see if he was still following her. She could see no sign of him and stopped to catch her breath, but the telltale sound of steel on wood alerted her to the fact that he was near and she ran on again.

She was now lost. She recognized none of the corridors. With their uniform doors they all seemed the same. She had hoped to run in a circle, reaching the stairs once Barker had left them, but she had no idea in which direction the stairs lay. The further she went, the more confused she became. She threaded her way through a further maze of passages. One of the cabins had its door open. Inside, sitting on the bottom bunk, were two men playing cards.

'Excuse me,' she gasped, holding her side as she stopped for a minute to catch her breath. 'How do I get to the deck from here?'

One of them muttered something unintelligible, waving his hands in the air. He must be foreign, she guessed. Her spirits fell. He had not understood a word she had said. Clutching her side, she went on.

Further down the corridor she saw another cabin with an open door. Again she asked for directions, and again she was met by a torrent of language she could not understand. She began to be seriously worried. The ship would be docking shortly. One way or another, she must find her way back to her stateroom.

The man continued talking and gesticulating, then, getting up, he pushed his way past her and went down the corridor. She would just have to ask someone else.

The stitch in her side had started to ease and she was about to hurry on when a voice called, 'Can I help you?'

Turning round, she saw the foreigner from the cabin. Next to him was another man.

'I'm Mr Müller, the steerage interpreter,' he said. He was a fine looking man with an air of solidity about him. Although he spoke with a heavy accent she had no difficulty in understanding him. 'Do you want something?'

'Oh, yes, thank you.' Emilia straightened up. She seemed to have lost her pursuer, and had finally found someone who could give her directions. Her fear began to leave her. 'I have lost my way. I need to get back to first class. If you can tell me the way to the deck, I can find my own way from there.'

'It's quite easy,' he said cheerfully. He gave her a series of instructions, finishing with: 'Then turn left, and you will find yourself at the stairs.'

She gave him a heartfelt thank you.

Hurriedly following his directions she found herself once more at the bottom of the staircase. And this time, there was no sign of Barker. Breathing a sigh of relief she picked up the hem of her dress and climbed the stairs to the poop deck. Never had a sight been more welcome. Although heavy smoke from the funnels was blowing across it, she made for it eagerly. Once outside, she would have no difficulty in returning to the first-class part of the deck, and then to her own stateroom.

She took in a deep breath as she emerged . . . only to see Barker scanning the deck. There was no use hiding. He had already seen her. And she would have to catch her breath before she could run any further.

'Well, well,' he said, advancing on her. 'If it isn't little Miss Cavendish.'

'What are you doing here?' she asked, backing away from him.

'I saw you getting on the ship. A pretty thing it would have been if I'd let you get away.'

'But how did you follow me? You didn't have a ticket,' she said in horror.

He grinned. 'So what? Plenty of other people on the dock did, all waving them round as they waited to get on board. All I had to do was stick a knife in someone's ribs and take his ticket, then when everyone crowded round him to see why he'd collapsed I slipped through the crowd and on to the boat.'

'No!' said Emilia in horror.

'You didn't think I'd let you go? I know better than that. Mr Montmorency would have had it out of my hide. He'll be mighty glad to know you're here, and he'll pay me a fortune when I give you to him. It's a pity I couldn't get you off at Cherbourg. I tried, but I couldn't get through to first class.' He spat. 'The stewards stopped me. Said I didn't belong there. I mustn't look life a toff,' he leered. 'But there's no one to stop me now, and I'll get you off at Queenstown instead. And then I can give you, right and tight, to Mr Montmorency.'

Emilia felt her stomach clench with fear.

'I don't see why you don't want him,' he said. 'He's rich, and he's besotted. He'll give you everything you want. You might as well make up your mind to it, because one way or another he's going to have you, and if you've any sense you'll let him have you with a ring on your finger instead of making him take you without. If he does that, you'll end up in the gutter, so why not come quietly?'

He reached out a hand and she dodged to the side, but in a whip-like movement he caught her wrist. 'You and I are going to spend the next few days together,' he said gloatingly, 'and when Mr Montmorency meets us in Ireland there'll be a tidy sum coming my way.'

'Let go of me,' she said, struggling to break free.

Barker only laughed, catching her round the waist and pinning her arms to her side.

Tired as she might be, Emilia still had plenty of spirit. With only her legs free, she stamped on his foot. Hard.

He gave a cry of pain and released his grip. It was only for a moment, but it was enough to allow her to break away. She ran . . . but saw too late that she was running straight towards the railings at the back of the ship, beyond which was nothing but the ocean. She heard his laughter behind her and her pulse started to race. She was trapped.

She looked round desperately for help but the cold wind had driven the rest of the third-class passengers below and the deck was empty. Barker walked toward her menacingly.

'Seems you've nowhere to go,' he said. 'Unless you fancy a jump into the blue yonder.'

She stood there with heart hammering as he approached her, knowing she had only one chance of escape. She waited until he was almost upon her, then darted past him, picking up her skirts as she ran across the poop deck, opening the gate that protected the top of the steps leading down to the aft deck and sprinting down them, then across the aft deck . . . and straight into the arms of Carl Latimer.

Four

She had never been so pleased to see anyone in her life. Arrogant Mr Latimer might be, but his strong, powerful body offered her protection, and she gave a sigh of gratitude for his presence.

His arms closed around her, and to her surprise she felt a tingling sensation starting from her shoulders and rippling right down to her feet. It was not unpleasant but it was unsettling, and it made her step back. She looked up, and met his eye. Just for a moment it was as though there was a connection between them. She felt powerfully drawn to him. So much so that she almost stepped forward, into his arms again.

Fortunately, she stopped herself just in time.

'There's no need to be in such a hurry,' he said, his eyes searching her face as he took her by the shoulders, steadying her, for she had not quite found her balance after running into him.

'No. Of course not.'

Only now did she realize how strange she must have looked, running along the deck as though the devil himself was after her. Which was not so very far from the truth . . . But still, it was no way to behave on an ocean liner.

She glanced instinctively over her shoulder to reassure herself, and was relieved when she could see no sign of Barker. The smoke from the funnels, blown by the wind, still obscured much of the poop deck, but in the ribbons of clean air in between she could see only empty deck.

He must have gone below. He would not want to provoke an open confrontation in front of witnesses, and as long as she could avoid him until she left the ship she should be safe.

She turned back to Mr Latimer . . . only to find that his eyes had followed hers and were now sweeping the deck.

'Has someone been bothering you?' he asked, turning to look at her in concern.

'No.' Her voice wobbled slightly, but she hoped he would not notice it. 'Why do you ask?' she asked, with what she believed was an expression of unconcern.

He looked at her searchingly, then said, 'No reason.'

She was relieved. She did not feel up to explaining the situation to Mr Latimer. She did not know him well enough to trust him. He continued to hold her gaze, however, and she began to feel uncomfortable, but fortunately he seemed to accept her word and offered her his arm.

She took it gratefully. She was still a little out of breath from running, and the stitch in her side had not yet gone, so she was grateful for his support. And not only for his support; the feel of his muscles through the fabric of his coat gave her a feeling of his strength, and she found it reassuring to know that he was by her side.

'I'm glad I've found you,' he said, as they went up the steps that led from the aft deck to the first-class deck.

He opened the gate for her at the top, then stood back to let her through. He followed her, closing the gate behind them, then once more offered her his arm.

'So am I,' was her heartfelt reply.

She bit her lip as soon as she had said it, but fortunately he didn't seem to notice her fervent tone of voice and he let it pass.

He made a few commonplace remarks, commenting on the weather and the size of the ship as they went back inside and headed towards her stateroom, but to her relief he did not seem to expect any kind of reply. Once they reached her stateroom, however, he dropped his pretence of cultivated courtesy and instead of leaving her at the door he said, 'Now, why don't you tell me what this is all about?'

'All what?' she asked, swallowing, as she turned to face him.

'You're shaking like a leaf. Something's upset you and I want to know what it is.'

'It's nothing. I'm cold, that's all, that's why I'm shaking. But I am below deck now, and will soon be better. Thank you, Mr Latimer, you have been most helpful.'

Her words had been intended as a dismissal, but when she went into her stateroom he followed her.

She turned to face him, and fixed a polite smile to her face. 'Mr Latimer, I'm grateful to you for the loan of your arm, but I'm afraid I must ask you to leave,' she said.

'All right, I will . . .'

She felt herself relax.

'Just as soon as you tell me what's bothering you,' he finished.

'Nothing's bothering me,' she said.

'Yes it is. What happened out there?' he asked.

'Nothing,' she said, unconsciously rubbing her hands together. 'I told you. I was shaking because of the cold.'

'Because you went out without a coat?' he asked.

'Yes.'

'And why did you do that?' he challenged her. 'It's April. No one in their right mind would take a walk on the deck without a coat on, which means you didn't intend to go outside. Something happened to you—'

'No, I do assure you . . .' she said, turning away from him and walking across the sitting room to the fireplace in an attempt to hide her agitation. She had thought she could fool him, but it was proving to be impossible, and the more he persisted the more uncomfortable she became.

She felt, rather than heard, him cross the stateroom behind her, then he took her by the shoulders and spun her gently to face him.

'The truth,' he said.

His voice was soft but insistent, and as he looked into her eyes, she knew she must make an effort to break away for him. If she did not, she would end up confiding in him, and that was something she did not want to do, because if she told him what had happened it would leave her exposed.

'Mr Latimer, it's none of your business,' she said firmly, stepping back, out of arm's reach.

'I'm making it my business,' he returned.

He let her go, but his eyes still followed her.

'Really, it was nothing,' she protested.

'Then why are you still on the ship?'

She raised her eyebrows. 'What do you mean?'

'You were supposed to disembark at Queenstown, but you didn't get off. The ship docked, then once the mail had been unloaded and the passengers had disembarked, it set off again. It left Ireland a quarter of an hour ago.'

'*What*?' she gasped.

'The ship has left Ireland. It is heading for New York.'

'Oh, no!'

She couldn't believe it. But a glance at the clock on the mantelpiece showed her that what he said was true.

She was devastated. All her plans had gone awry. She had been lost for much longer than she had realized, and she was now trapped on the ship. Even worse, she was trapped with Barker, and she would be until they reached New York.

'It must have been something pretty bad to make you lose all track of time like that,' he went on.

'Yes . . . no . . .' she stammered.

He walked towards her and put his finger under her chin, lifting it so that she was looking into his eyes.

'You're still shivering.'

There was something caring in his voice that made her heart stand still. It was mellifluous, deep and rich; she found it hypnotic, and against her will she felt herself weakening.

'I'm . . .'

'And don't tell me you're cold. The stateroom's heated, and I won't believe you.'

'Mr Latimer, do you always cross examine your fellow travellers?' she asked, stepping back and trying to make light of things, though inside she was almost at her wits' end with worry.

'No. My fellow travellers rarely interest me. But you do.'

The stateroom seemed suddenly too small. Despite the fact

she had taken two steps back he still seemed alarmingly near. He was not a very tall man – no more than five feet ten or five feet eleven inches – but his personality was so large and his presence so strong that it seemed to fill the room. She had never met a man like him before. He annoyed her and exasperated her, but at the same time he set her nerve endings on fire.

Taking a hold of herself, she felt she must give him some explanation for her nervous state. Not the real one, of course. Confiding in him would make her vulnerable. And vulnerable was one thing she did not want to be around Carl Latimer.

She straightened her shoulders and smoothed her skirt, then said, 'I lost my way. I wanted to explore the rest of the ship before leaving it, and somehow I found myself in steerage. I tried to find my way out again, but the corridors were all the same and I became anxious. I twisted and turned, trying to find my way up on to the deck, before realizing I was lost.'

'And you were worried about being unable to find your way back to first class in time to get off the ship?' he asked, looking into her eyes as though he could read the truth written there.

'Yes,' she said.

She returned his gaze. It was, after all, partly true, even if it wasn't the whole truth.

'I see.'

Whether he believed her or not she could not tell, but he said no more.

'If the ship has already left Ireland then I have no choice but to remain aboard,' she said, sinking into a chair.

'No. Like it or not, you're bound for New York.'

'My poor godmother. When I don't arrive at her house as arranged, she will be sick with worry. I have no way of letting her know what has happened. Oh! It is too unfortunate.'

'It's not as bad as you think,' he said, pulling up a chair and sitting down opposite her. 'There's a telegraph office on board the ship—'

'A telegraph office?' she asked in surprise. 'On board *Titanic*?'

He nodded. 'Yes. You can telegraph your godmother and let her know what has happened.'

She felt a huge flood of relief. 'Oh, what a good idea. It will be the very thing. As long as she knows I'm safe, she won't be concerned.'

'Would you like me to show you the way?' he asked.

A part of her wanted to refuse his offer but another part of her was wary of wandering round the ship alone.

'Thank you.'

He looked at her curiously.

'Is anything wrong?' she asked.

'No. Not really. It's just that I didn't expect you to agree so easily.'

'Why not? It's very kind of you.'

'Kind?'

'Yes. Kind,' she said.

He looked puzzled, as though he found her difficult to understand. Nevertheless, he offered his arm, and together they went to the telegraph office.

It was a hive of activity. Passengers were queuing to send messages to their friends and families, and Emilia had to wait her turn. At last she was able to compose a simple telegram to her godmother, explaining that a mishap had prevented her from disembarking at Queenstown, but promising that she would wire again from New York when she knew what her new date of arrival would be.

'It was fortunate for me that you were walking on deck when you were,' she remarked as they left the telegraph office.

'There was nothing fortunate about it. I was looking for you,' he said with a wry smile.

'Oh?' she enquired. Then suddenly she remembered the circumstances of their last meeting, and she felt herself flush as she recalled how she had meddled in his mother's affairs, thereby causing that poor lady to collapse on the stairs. Her face fell. 'Oh,' she said again. This time the word came out on a drooping note. 'I must apologize,' she said, trying to meet his eye and not quite succeeding. 'I had no right to interfere. It was unpardonable of me.'

'No, not unpardonable.'

His voice was teasing. Surprised, she looked up to see that there was a gleam of warmth in his eyes.

'Quite the opposite, in fact,' he remarked. 'I'm glad you did.'

'Glad?' She was surprised. 'But my interference led your mother to collapse.'

'Ah. I see you are under a misapprehension. It's the same misapprehension I was suffering from when I spoke to you so angrily – for which I hope you will forgive me. My mother didn't collapse,' he explained, 'she simply hadn't found her sea legs.'

'Then she was not ill?' asked Emilia, her hopes rising.

'Far from it. She is better than I've seen her for years. She hadn't managed to go very far before her legs refused to do as she wanted them to, but even so she had seen a wide range of new sights and sounds which had stimulated her, and aroused her interest in life.'

He was smiling down at her. The hard lines round his mouth and eyes had softened, making him look very appealing, and Emilia realized just how attractive he was. Not in a classical way, for his face was too decided for masculine beauty, but nevertheless his firm jaw, strong cheekbones and high brow were handsome in a vigorous way.

She smiled back. 'I'm glad. I felt so guilty. I thought I'd done her a great deal of harm. But if she's truly well enough to be out, then I'm sure the wonders of the ship will lift her spirits.'

'I have promised to show her round this afternoon and she's already looking forward to it. But first she wanted me to find you and thank you for what you had done. She wanted me to ask you to dine with us this evening. At the time, I thought it would be impossible, but as it is . . .'

She said nothing. She felt an unaccountable drop in her spirits because he had sought her out, not on his own account, but on his mother's. And yet why should that lower her spirits?

'I'm afraid I wasn't very friendly at our previous meetings,' he continued, 'but can we not put that behind us? We will have to endure each other's company for a few more days on board ship, and it will be a lot pleasanter if we can be on good terms.'

His charm was very hard to resist. Besides, what he said was true. They would in all probability meet each other a number of times over the next few days and it would not do to be on bad terms.

'Very well,' she said with a smile.

'Then you will dine with us?'

'Yes, thank you, I will.' A sudden thought struck her. 'Oh, dear, now that I'm to stay aboard until we reach New York, your mother won't be able to make use of my stateroom for the rest of the journey.'

'It doesn't matter,' he said with a shrug. 'She's feeling so much better that she will be able to go out and about, and will not feel cramped or shut in where she is.'

She felt a relaxing of a knot inside her as she realized that Mr Latimer had accepted defeat, and he had done so with a good grace. Rich though he was, he did not pursue his own goals at all costs. Perhaps he was not as much to be feared as she supposed. But that did not mean she could drop her guard entirely. Wealthy men were used to getting their own way, and she must not make the mistake of thinking that he was safe just because he no longer wanted her stateroom. There was a streak of ruthlessness in him that it would be perilous for her to ignore.

Still, she could not help looking forward to dinner – although she still had one thing to worry her: what on earth should she wear?

That question was still vexing her that evening, as she was preparing to go to the dining room. She had only three evening gowns, and none of them were suitable. She had worn a home-made dress the evening before, thinking that as long as she sat at an inconspicuous table no one would notice, but it had drawn forth a number of cutting comments from some of the ladies in the dining room. She did not want to embarrass Carl, and so she knew she must not wear it again. But her other two gowns were scarcely any better. Both of them had belonged to her Aunt Clem, and were five years behind the times. There was a yellow satin or a green silk. In the end she decided on the silk. Its waist sat on the natural waist line, instead of following the fashionable Empire line and sitting beneath the breasts, and its skirt was fuller than was presently fashionable, but it was very beautiful. A sudden inspiration hit her. If she tied a sash round the waist, making it wide enough to reach to just beneath her breasts, it would make the gown appear to be high-waisted, and as sashes were very fashionable at the moment it would also add a contemporary look to the gown. The one from her home-made dress would not do as the colour would clash, but by good fortune she possessed a white silk scarf which could pass for a sash.

Having settled the problem to her satisfaction she luxuriated in a scented bath, then stepped into her cotton underwear and slipped on the gown, which rustled as it fell into place. She was just wondering how to fasten it when her stewardess, Mrs McLaren, called to see if she had everything she needed.

'Could you help me fasten my dress?' Emilia asked, grateful to see the stewardess.

'Of course, miss. What a beautiful gown,' said Mrs McLaren as she fastened it. 'I'm so pleased you decided not to get off at Queenstown,' she carried on, blissfully unaware of the real reason behind Emilia's change of plans. 'I think you're right to take this opportunity to see New York. It's a wonderful place.'

To explain the fact that she had not left the ship, Emilia had said she had changed her mind about disembarking in Ireland. As the stateroom had been booked for the entire journey there was fortunately no problem about her remaining on board.

'Would you like me to help you with your hair, miss?' asked Mrs McLaren.

'Oh, yes, please, could you?' Emilia replied.

She sat down in front of the dressing table whilst Mrs McLaren brushed her hair, then braided small sections before wrapping them round the bulk of hair, which was arranged in a loose chignon.

Emilia thanked her.

'Not at all, miss,' she said, before leaving to attend to her other passengers.

When she had gone, Emilia brushed a few small waves around her face to soften the style, and combed the golden tendrils that were too short to fit into the chignon, but which nestled in the nape of her neck, making them tidy. Then she picked up a string of pearls from the dressing table and held them against her. The necklace had belonged to her mother, and was the only piece of jewellery she possessed. She wondered whether to fasten it round her chignon, as was currently fashionable, or whether to wear it around her neck.

At last she decided to wear it round her neck. It was not really long enough to wrap round her chignon, and besides, her throat looked bare without something to adorn it.

Having finished with her hair, she went over to the wardrobe and took out her scarf, winding it round the dress to create a high-waisted effect, and was pleased with the result. Then, pulling on her evening gloves – also inherited from Aunt Clem – she was ready to go.

The ship was ablaze with light as she made her way to the dining room. It shimmered and shone from electric fittings that were disguised as candlesticks and flambeaux . And it was not only the lights that shone. The jewels round the necks, wrists and throats of the ladies shone, too. A ship of millionaires, *Titanic* had been called, and Emilia could well believe it. She had never seen so many jewels. They adorned people she had seen only in the newspapers: Colonel and Mrs Astor, Benjamin Guggenheim, and the Countess of Rothes, all of whom looked splendid. Then there was Isador Strauss, joint owner of Macy's department store in New York, with his wife Ida. They were an elderly couple, but appeared to be very loving. In fact, the passengers were almost a who's who of the wealthy, the well connected and the fashionable.

The area was so crowded that she was just beginning to wish she had made more detailed arrangements for meeting Mr Latimer, when a voice beside her said, 'May I?' and there was Mr Latimer offering her his arm.

His dark hair was fashionably slicked back over his head, and was gleaming in the brilliant electric light. In his evening clothes, he was looking extremely attractive. His white shirt with its wing collar, white waistcoat and bow tie, together with the white flower in his buttonhole, set off the light olive of his complexion. His black tailcoat was superbly moulded to his broad shoulders, and his well-cut trousers showed the length and firmness of his legs.

So well did he look that she felt momentarily uncomfortable in her aunt's old gown, but she saw there was no disparagement in his eyes. Instead, there was an unmistakeable admiration which filled her with a warm glow.

She accepted his arm with a smile and they went into the dining room. The sound of chatter and laughter mingled with the strains of the ship's orchestra, which was playing light classical music. Their stringed instruments provided the perfect backdrop to the opulent setting. Large leaded light windows were set at either side of the room and tall white columns supported the moulded ceilings, whilst gold light fittings flooded the room with light.

He led her over to a large table in the middle of the dining room. Sparkling crystal glasses and silver cutlery gleamed on spotless white tablecloths, which were decorated with a mass of flowers.

As they passed Mr and Mrs Gisborne's table, Mr Gisborne said to his wife, 'You'd better tell your sister to look lively if she wants to make sure of Latimer for Isabelle. It seems to me he's smitten with that young girl. Not surprised, either. She's a damn fine filly.'

'Don't be coarse,' said his wife mechanically.

'She must be well connected, too,' he said, unperturbed. 'She's in the Branchester's stateroom. They had to cancel at the last minute. The girl must be a protégé of theirs.'

'She's nothing of the kind. I had the full story from Charlotte. She and Edward had to cancel their trip, and she offered the stateroom to an old school friend of hers, an impoverished woman of no family living in Ireland. Her friend could not make use of it, but her friend's goddaughter could. And that is who the young girl is: Miss Cavendish, the goddaughter of one of Charlotte's old school friends,' she said contemptuously.

'Even so, she's a good looking girl,' he said, putting his cigar back into his mouth.

'She's little more than tolerable,' remarked his wife.

However, the sight of Carl and Emilia together disturbed her. It was not the first time that she had been made aware of the fact that Carl Latimer was showing an interest in one of the female passengers. A good friend of hers, Mrs de Brett, had dropped her a hint of it over breakfast. If it was a shipboard dalliance on his part, a momentary indulgence to pass the time until the ship reached New York, then she had no objection to it. But if it should turn out to be more serious, she had a great objection indeed. He was as good as engaged to her niece, and she wasn't about to let him escape the hook when Isabelle was so close to landing him.

Seeing Miss Cavendish, Mrs Gisborne had been somewhat reassured. The girl was beautiful, it was true, but she had none of the polish of Isabelle, and could bring Carl nothing in the way of status or contacts. What's more, he was smart enough to know it. His money had bought him into society, but only breeding and a link with an old family name could open the last few doors. And as family names went, Isabelle had one of the oldest.

Still, the situation bore watching. Miss Cavendish appeared to be unaware of his interest, but that could be a pose. If she was a scheming hussy, instead of the simple girl she appeared, she might try and get her hooks into Carl before she left the ship. That was a situation Mrs Gisborne would have to be prepared for.

An idea began to form at the back of her mind. She had in her possession a certain magazine containing a society photograph of Carl which could be put to good account. If she left it in a prominent position in her stateroom, then if ever she should have need of it she could send a note to her maid, via one of the stewards, to bring it to her. The photograph was

51

accompanied by a caption which would put an end to Miss Cavendish's pretensions once and for all.

Emilia was enjoying herself. To begin with, she had been overwhelmed by the splendour of her surroundings, but she had quickly relaxed and was now having a wonderful time.

'Now isn't this nice, all of us having dinner together? I wanted to say thank you, dear, for coming into my cabin like that yesterday,' said Mrs Latimer to Emilia.

She looked so different that Emilia could hardly believe it was the same lady. Gone was the grey skin and worried expression. In their place was an alert look and sparkling eyes. Her dress, too, showed her better spirits. It was not black, but dark blue, and shone with sequins.

'I'm so glad you are feeling better,' said Emilia.

'So am I. I never thought I'd end up eating in the dining room. My stewardess is a good woman and brought me a bite to eat on a tray, but it isn't like sitting here and watching the world go by.'

'Oh, no,' sighed Miss Epson, her companion. 'This is so much nicer.'

'We'll be having some guests to dine with us,' said Mr Latimer. 'I'm very lucky they agreed to join us. They're much sought after, as you can imagine. Ah, here's my first guest now.'

He stood up as a fine looking gentleman with dark hair and a luxuriant moustache approached. Like the other gentlemen, he was resplendent in evening dress, with black trousers and tailcoat, and a white shirt, waistcoat and bow tie.

'May I present Mr Bruce Ismay,' he said. 'Mr Ismay, my mother, Mrs Latimer; her companion, Miss Epson; and Miss Cavendish.'

Mr Ismay greeted them charmingly before taking his place at the table.

'Mr Ismay is the managing director and chairman of the White Star Line,' said Mr Latimer.

'Oh, how wonderful!' exclaimed Miss Epson, clasping her hands together and looking at Mr Ismay with admiration.

'You must be very proud of your beautiful ship,' said Mrs Latimer.

'We are,' he said. 'She's the pride of the White Star Line. Everyone who has worked on her has surpassed themselves, from the engineers to the carpenters. But you should not be congratulating me, you know. It's Andrews you should be congratulating. He built her.'

Emilia turned in the direction of his eyes and saw Mr Andrews heading towards the table.

'Andrews. Good of you to join us,' said Mr Latimer.

'Not at all. The pleasure's all mine,' he said.

'We were just saying what a wonderful ship *Titanic* is,' said Emilia. 'Mr Ismay was telling us we must not compliment him, but that we must direct our compliments to you, as you built her.'

Mr Andrews smiled. 'Not singlehandedly,' he said.

'Mr Andrews is very fond of his ship. He calls it his baby,' said Mr Ismay. 'Do you know, before we set sail, he spent the best part of every day on *Titanic*, not leaving until half past six in the evening. He put every rack, table, chair, and electric fan in place himself.'

'*Almost* every one,' he said.

There was general laughter.

'Well, she's a credit to you,' said Mr Latimer. 'I've travelled on *Olympic* before, but she's nothing compared to *Titanic*. This ship is a marvel.'

'And so she should be,' said Mr Ismay, as they perused the menu. 'It's taken us three years to build her, almost to the day.'

'Do you always travel on the maiden voyages, or did you make a special case of *Titanic*, Mr Ismay?' asked Emilia, once the waiter had taken their order.

'I always take the first trip on any new ship,' said Mr Ismay. 'I like to see what improvements we can make for the next ship we're building. Take *Titanic*, for example. I came up with a number of ideas for her whilst travelling on *Olympic*'s maiden voyage. It was then that I had the idea of putting a covered trellis café overlooking the ocean on board *Titanic*.'

'That would be the Café Parisien,' said Mrs Latimer. 'Carl and I took tea there earlier today.'

'A truly wonderful ship,' said Carl. He raised his glass. 'Here's to *Titanic*, and all who sail in her.'

The other members of his party raised their glasses in the toast. '*Titanic!*' they chorused.

Their soup arrived and they turned their attention to it, but when the plates had been cleared, Emilia asked, 'How much longer will we be at sea?'

'For another five days,' said Mr Ismay. 'We hope to reach New York on Wednesday morning.'

Emilia found herself looking forward to the journey. The splendour of the surroundings had driven all thoughts of her frightening encounter with Barker from her mind and she was thinking only of spending five more days on *Titanic*. And five more days with Mr Latimer.

He was sitting opposite her at the table, and although she took her share in the conversation, she was constantly aware of him. He had a strong presence, one that made her heart beat faster whenever he was near.

They continued to talk about the great ship throughout dinner, which was served on magnificent Crown Derby china, but once it was over the conversation turned to the orchestra. They were playing delightfully, adding a cultured atmosphere to the evening.

'I see you got Hartley for the trip,' said Mr Latimer, glancing towards the leader of the orchestra.

'Yes,' said Mr Ismay. 'He's an excellent musician. We're lucky to have him. In fact, the whole orchestra's excellent.'

A number of couples were taking to the dance floor.

Mr Latimer turned to Emilia and said, 'Would you care to dance?'

She shouldn't, she knew that. She had been enjoying Mr Latimer's company during dinner, but she was becoming aware she was enjoying it too much. Not only was she constantly aware of him, but she found him intriguing. He mixed easily with people from the most exalted walks of life, and yet he bore the unmistakeable stamp of someone who had pulled himself up from nothing. She wondered what the early experiences of his life had been, not only to allow him to rise in such a way, but to allow him to have such assurance once he had done so.

'No, thank you . . .' she began.

'Oh, don't say no,' said Mrs Latimer. 'I want to see Carl dance. He never usually asks anyone. Do it to please me, dear.'

Thus entreated, Emilia felt it would be rude to refuse again, and reluctantly she stood up.

'Is it really so bad, having to dance with me?' he murmured, as he led her out on to the floor, guiding her past waiters and other dancers.

She flushed. 'No, not at all.'

'And yet you were going to refuse me,' he said, as he took her hand in his own. 'Why?'

She could not tell him the real reason, that the thought of dancing filled her with a confusing mixture of anticipation and apprehension.

'I-I've eaten too much!' she laughed.

To her relief, he laughed, too. But then he said, 'I don't believe you.'

The change in him was so sudden that she felt her heart skip a beat.

'I beg your pardon?' she said.

He looked down into her eyes. 'I said, I don't believe you.'

His gaze was intense, and it made her breathless.

'You're not supposed to say that,' she remarked, flustered.

'I know. But I rarely do what I'm supposed to do. So why don't you tell me what you were thinking?' he said, as he slipped his arm round her waist.

She could feel the heat of his hand as it came to rest in the small of her back, and as he pulled her closer she began to tingle from head to foot.

He had asked her a question, but his nearness had driven it from her mind. She was conscious of nothing but the heat of his body so close to her own, and the soft whisper of his breath against her cheek. It felt like a warm wind, making her instinctively lift her face to his.

He smiled down into her eyes, but there was something predatory in the smile. And yet she did not feel threatened by it. Rather, she felt exhilarated.

'Well?' he asked.

His voice was deep and throaty. It sent tingles up and down her spine.

'I have forgotten the question,' she said.

His smile broadened, and the pressure of his hand became more intense. 'Have you? But I've only just asked it.'

'There are so many distractions. The music, the people, the . . . .' *Feel of your arm round me*, she thought, but could not say it.

She did not need to. By the look in his eyes, it seemed as though he could read her mind.

'I asked you what you were thinking,' he said, as he began to whirl her round the floor.

He was a good dancer, light on his feet and yet firm in his touch. He guided her effortlessly between the other couples on the floor.

Lulled by the familiar rhythm and steps of the waltz, Emilia at last felt able to reply. All she said, however, was, 'I really can't remember.'

'Yes, you can.'

She swallowed. Then looked up into his eyes.

'Very well,' she said. 'I was wondering what experiences you must have had in your early life to make you the man you are today.'

He raised his eyebrows. 'And what exactly is "the man I am today"?'

She bit her lip, but then said resolutely, 'A man who is the equal of anyone here, though he wasn't born to wealth or position.'

'Ah. You noticed,' he said teasingly.

She smiled. 'Yes. I did.'

He laughed. 'You're right. My beginnings were very different to this.'

He glanced round the opulent dining room, with its flower-laden tables, sparkling glasses, gleaming silver, glittering lights and its immaculate guests. Then his expression changed, and just for a moment she caught sight of something that lurked beneath the surface, a boy driven by need and want, clawing his way out of difficulties to be in a position where he could sail on the finest ship in the world, on terms of equality with some of its wealthiest and most well-connected people.

'Yes?' she prompted him.

He gave a wry smile. 'It isn't fit for a lady's ears.'

'I'm not a lady,' she returned.

'I beg to differ,' he said, suddenly serious. Just for a moment he stopped whirling her round the floor. In the midst of the other dancers they were still. 'I've met females of every type and rank, and you are definitely a lady.'

She flushed. 'I was born that way, and perhaps you are right, in all the ways that matter, I am one still, but I am not a hothouse flower. I have seen my share of hardship and I would like to know what drives you.'

'Very well,' he said. His hand pressed more firmly into the small of her back and, holding her in his arms, he resumed the dance. 'My family lived in a poor neighbourhood in Southampton, struggling to survive. My mother took in washing and went scrubbing floors for a few coppers to help feed us – there were eleven of us, all told. My father worked on the docks. When I was twelve he was crippled in an accident and couldn't work. I did what I could, making myself useful, running errands, making coppers. And then one day I found a bicycle. It was bent and rusty, and had been abandoned in an alleyway.'

He broke off as he whirled her expertly past two other couples.

'I mended it,' he continued, 'and used it to help me ply my trade. I delivered parcels quickly and I could go further afield than the boys on foot. By attaching a cart to my bicycle I could carry more parcels. Bit by bit, I built up a business. As soon as I could afford it I bought an old motor van. It was broken down but I repaired it. I was just starting to make some headway when my father died. He had been ill for years, but it hit my mother hard. She was still taking in washing;

still scrubbing floors. She took to her bed for a few days after my father died, knocked down by grief. The ladies she cleaned for gave her notice. They said she was unreliable.' His hand gripped her own more tightly. 'She'd been working for them for ten years.'

She heard the hard edge in his voice, and knew how much it had affected him, that his mother should be so badly treated.

'It doesn't seem to have made you bitter,' she said. Although his voice had been hard, there had been no bitterness in it. 'You could have started to hate those with wealth, resenting them for everything they had, but you didn't.'

'I can't see the point in bitterness. It's destructive. I channelled my disgust, using it to make me work harder than ever. I bought more vans. Eventually I had a whole fleet of them. Once the business was doing well I put it in the charge of my brother and travelled to America. I had heard great things about it; that it was a land of opportunity. I quickly saw it was somewhere I could achieve even greater things. I set up a similar business, and once it was established I moved my family over there with me. I sold the English business and used the profits to help my brothers and sisters. Of course, I made sure my mother never had to go back to scrubbing floors again. I hired someone to scrub her floor; then someone to do the heavy housework for her, then the light housework, then someone to fetch and carry. It's a strange thing,' he said. 'First, my money saved her from drudgery, but then it stopped her having to do anything at all.'

'And that is why she became ill?' ventured Emilia.

'I didn't realize it at the time, but yes, I think it is.'

'Not having enough to do is as bad as having too much to do,' she said.

He nodded. Tightening his grip on her hand a little, and resetting his hand on the small of her back, he guided her round the edge of the dance floor. The effect of his slight change in his grasp was to make her aware of him all over again. She had waltzed before on the rare occasions when her parents had entertained. She had only been eighteen at the time, but her parents had thought it would be good for her to gain some social experience and develop some poise. They had hosted a number of social evenings, and she had danced with the young men from round about. But they had never made her feel alive in their arms; expectant; as though she was waiting for something. Their grips had been firm, their dancing assured. With them, a waltz had been a dance. With Carl it was something more. Much more.

He was speaking again. She recalled her thoughts and focused on what he was saying.

'I made the mistake of trying to shelter my mother from everything,' he said, 'and ended up sheltering her from life itself. Until you came along, standing up to me.' He looked down into her eyes as the music came to an end. 'You're a very remarkable person, Emilia.'

'I don't think you should call me that,' she said, suddenly self-conscious. It made her afraid. If once she let Carl Latimer close to her, she did not think she would have the strength to push him away again.

'No. I know I shouldn't,' he said huskily. 'But I want to. And I would like you to call me Carl.'

She must not contemplate it, even for a moment. It was true, she already thought of him as Carl, but to call him by his first name, to say it out loud, would be unthinkable. It would produce an intimacy that would be threatening to her peace of mind.

'It's out of the question,' she said, pulling away from him.

He held on to her hand, so that she was forced to turn back towards him.

'You wondered what had turned me into the person I am today,' he said, 'and I have told you. But I have wondered the same about you. What gave you the courage to stand up to me the way you did? What made you interfere when you heard my mother's wistful voice? I've made a journey from poverty to wealth, but I have a feeling you've made a journey the other way. Yet, like me, it has not made you bitter.'

'Carl,' came a voice at their elbows.

Emilia saw his face darken. Nevertheless, he turned round politely.

'Adlington,' he said.

Emilia saw a distinguished-looking gentleman with grey hair who was dressed in immaculate evening clothes. On his arm was an equally distinguished, grey-haired lady, who was wearing a dress by Paul Poiret, and who was dripping with diamonds.

'I didn't know you were on board,' said Mr Adlington to Carl. 'What a pleasant surprise. We haven't seen enough of you lately. Have we, Victoria?'

'No, indeed we haven't,' said his wife.

'Will we be seeing you and Isabelle at the Jannson's party when we get to New York?' asked Mr Adlington.

Isabelle? thought Emilia. Who is Isabelle?

She had no time to worry about it, however, because a voice at her own elbow claimed her attention.

'Miss Cavendish?'

She turned to see a beautifully-dressed woman in early middle age, whom she knew to be Mrs Gisborne, as she had heard the waiter addressing the lady by that name.

'I hope you will forgive me taking such a liberty, but I felt I ought to give you a word of warning,' said Mrs Gisborne, taking Emilia's arm and leading her from the dance floor. Emilia would have resisted, but Mrs Gisborne's next word arrested her attention. 'Carl is such an attractive man, and I can see you are not immune to his charm, so I feel I must put you on your guard.'

She allowed herself to be led from the dance floor, feeling apprehensive.

'It is as well to know the truth, before anyone comes to harm,' said Mrs Gisborne, slipping a magazine into her hand. Then, bowing, she moved away.

Emilia glanced down at the magazine. It was open at the society pages. There, staring back at her, was a photograph of Carl. He was looking relaxed and happy in the midst of a group of young people. Beneath the photograph was a caption:

A happy alliance. A rumour has reached this magazine that
an interesting announcement is shortly to take place concerning

Titanic Affair

Mr Carl Latimer, lately of England, and Miss Isabelle Stott, the dazzling adornment of one of the oldest families in Boston. They will unite their two countries, as well as their persons, with a formal engagement, which will be announced as soon as Mr Latimer returns from Europe.

Emilia's limbs went weak, and she sank down in a chair, her eyes tracing and retracing the photograph of Carl and Isabelle. They would be announcing their engagement when he returned from a business trip to Europe. Even now, he was as good as engaged.

Feeling suddenly sick, she was about to slip out of the dining room, when she realized how rude it would be of her to leave without saying goodnight. Unable to face Carl, she returned to the table, making her excuses to his mother.

'Sea sickness?' Mrs Latimer asked sympathetically. 'You look a bit pale, dear. Don't worry, I'll tell Carl you've gone to bed.'

Relieved that her sudden absence did not seem rude, Emilia left the dining room once again. Tears pricked at the back of her eyes as she hurried through public rooms and down narrow corridors until she finally reached her stateroom. She opened the door with trembling fingers, and gratefully closed it behind her.

She stood leaning back against the door. She had been having such a marvellous evening, and then suddenly, everything had collapsed.

She had thought . . . What? she asked herself angrily, as she pushed herself away from the door and went into the bedroom, throwing the magazine down angrily before sitting down at the dressing table and unpinning her hair. What had she thought? That he was attracted to her? That he liked her? That he more than liked her? Yes. And why?

Because of her feelings for him.

She had been aware of a growing connection with him throughout the evening as he had revealed details of his past, and she had thought that connection was mutual. She now realized she had been wrong. Carl had no feelings for her. He had told her about his past because she had asked him to, and as for taking her in his arms, he had done it because it was a requirement of the waltz.

Thank goodness she had discovered the truth in time. Now that she knew, she could fight her attraction, she thought, as she began to brush her loosened hair. He might be the most interesting man she had ever met, and he might be the most attractive; he might make her tremble from head to foot when he took her into his arms, but he was beyond her reach.

Her course was clear, she thought, as her hands stilled. She must be at pains to avoid him. It was only for a few days. It should not be too difficult. Now that he had thanked her for helping his mother he would have no reason to seek her out, in which case it was unlikely their paths would cross. Though they were on a ship, it was large, and it should not be impossible to avoid him. It would only be for a few days, and then she would be landing in New York.

She would send a telegraph to Charlie Potter, she decided, remembering that Freddy had told her of their friend's removal to America. Now that she had been compelled to visit New York she would make the most of it, and she hoped she would be able to see him before setting sail for Ireland. She would like to know how he was getting on in the antiques trade, and perhaps she would also be able to meet Julia. And Charlie, she hoped, would be able to advise her on cheap but respectable lodgings, so that she would have somewhere comfortable to stay until she could book her return passage.

Once in Ireland with her godmother, it would be easy to forget Carl Latimer, she told herself. She would have a new life opening out in front of her, and she would soon put him out of her mind.

That, at least was the theory. But she was uncomfortably aware that it was not going to be so simple in practise.

Five

Carl sat in the smoking room with a glass of brandy in his hand.

It was now two hours since Emilia had made her excuses to his mother and returned to her stateroom. He had seen her leaving across the dining room but, being tied up in conversation, he had been unable to stop her. By the time he had disentangled himself, she had gone. He had wanted to follow her, but on his mother telling him that she had been feeling sea sick he had reluctantly let her go. He had seen his mother back to her room and then he had retired to the smoking room. But whilst the conversations about politics and business swirled all around him, he did not hear a word of what was being said.

Forty-eight hours ago it would have been a different story. He would have been leading the conversation, not ignoring it. But since then much had changed. So much so, that he was no longer the same man who had boarded the ship in Southampton. And all because of Emilia Cavendish. She had challenged his most deeply held beliefs and shown him they were nothing more than paper blowing in the wind.

How had she done it? he wondered, as he took a drink of brandy and lit a cigar. How had one slight slip of a girl managed to change his opinion so radically on such a number of important subjects?

He thought back to their first encounter, when he had offered to buy her stateroom.

'Money can't buy everything', she had told him, and he had not believed her. But she had been right. It had not been able to buy everything – or indeed anything, as far as Emilia was concerned. It had been unable to buy her stateroom for his mother. And it had been unable to buy her good opinion. It was then he had realized that money was not the magic wand he had long believed it to be.

It wasn't that he now underestimated its power. Far from it. He knew what money could do. It had saved him and his family from a life of grinding poverty, and it had provided food for his mother, his father and his nine brothers and sisters.

Sadly, their number had now dwindled to seven. Infant mortality was the darkest side of poverty: children dying for lack of hygienic living conditions and medical care. Both Will and Ellen had died of pneumonia: his rise to fortune had come too late for them. But not too late for Sarah, Harry, Vicky, Martha, Ted, Gus and John. They were all now leading comfortable lives. Sarah and Vicky were married and, thanks to his fortune, had pleasant houses in a leafy suburb, with clean air for the children to breathe and servants to help them around the house. Harry, Ted and Gus had set up their own businesses, and were doing very well. John, with his help, had trained to be a doctor, and Martha was training to be a nurse.

No, he wasn't in any danger of underestimating money and the power it wielded, but, until he had met Emilia, he had overestimated it. It had taken her to remind him of its true worth.

'What do you think of this feud between Roosevelt and Taft, Latimer?' asked one of the other gentlemen.

The question broke in on his thoughts. He took a sip of brandy, mentally reviewing the portions of conversation he had overheard and realizing the political situation was under discussion. There was a long-standing feud between ex-President Theodore Roosevelt and President William Taft. Both were able and gifted men, but both had strong opinions and conflict was inevitable.

'I think it's been going on for far too long,' he said.

'Hear, hear. They ought to sort their differences out,' the gentlemen agreed.

A range of opinions broke out amongst the other gentlemen, and he was free to return to his thoughts.

It was not only in his view of money that she had changed him; she had made him see other aspects of his life in a different light. When he had boarded the ship a few short days before, he had been contemplating marriage to one of the well-connected but impoverished young ladies to whom he was constantly being introduced.

Miss Miranda Pargeter was one of them. Miss Pargeter came from a powerful family with political connections, and would have provided him with an elegant and intelligent wife. She was good looking and immaculately dressed, and a marriage to her would have given him influential contacts if he had had a mind run for election at some future date.

Then there had been Miss Isabelle Stott. Miss Stott's family were old and well-connected, with entrées into every level of society. Ordinarily, they would have considered him beneath them, but their fortunes had suffered a reverse in recent times and they were actively looking for a wealthy husband for Isabelle. Not that they had admitted their poverty, of course. They had at all times kept up appearances. But he had looked into their circumstances and discovered that they were almost bankrupt. That, he assumed, was the reason for them leaking news of a 'forthcoming engagement' with Isabelle to one of the society magazines, in an effort to force his hand. It hadn't worked. But he had still considered Isabelle as a possible wife.

And then there had been Miss Olive Theakston. Miss Theakston's family had had a different reason for wishing for an alliance. Miss Theakston's father was, like him, a self-made man, and a marriage between the two families would have smoothed the way for a business merger between the two businesses. It would have been very lucrative for all concerned.

They were all elegant, refined and intelligent young women; all suitable matches. And all women he had been contemplating spending the rest of his life with when he'd boarded the ship.

And then he had met Emilia, and his ideas had undergone

a radical change. She was unimpressed by his wealth. She did not react to it. Instead, she reacted to him, as a man. Arguing with him, berating him, teasing him, laughing with him . . . But that was not the whole of it. Not only was she unimpressed by his wealth, she was someone he could admire and respect. Her own life had been far from easy. He did not yet know what had reduced her to her present state of poverty, but it must have been difficult for her to leave a life of comfort and descend to the level of having to wear home-made clothes. And yet there was no trace of self-pity or bitterness in her. He admired her for it, as he admired her for the way she had stood up to him, defending the needs of an elderly lady she did not even know. He respected her for sticking to her principles and refusing to sell her stateroom, no matter what the temptation. And he enjoyed her company. He could not remember when he had ever enjoyed anyone's company more.

Then there were the feelings of protectiveness that she brought out in him with her softness and her vulnerability. When she had run into his arms on deck, he had wanted to shield her from whatever it was that had frightened her.

He finished his brandy.

It no longer seemed enticing to marry into one of the first families of America, adding his wealth to an old name and thereby creating a powerful union, or to marry in order to cement a business merger which would result in yet more millions. Both ideas, which had been a source of such interest to him only a few days before, now left him cold.

Emilia woke early. She had not slept well. The evening before had been full of conflicting emotions. First of all she had been intensely drawn to Carl Latimer, and then she had discovered that he was engaged, or as good as engaged, to Miss Isabelle Stott. The shock had hit her with surprising force. On seeing the magazine, the strength had ebbed out of her as though she had received a physical blow. Why her feelings for him were so strong she did not know. It was true she found him both attractive and intriguing, but she had known him for such a short space of time that she should have been able to put him out of her mind. But such had not been the case. He had haunted her waking thoughts, and when she had at last fallen asleep he had filled her dreams.

Still, it was a new day and, rising quickly, she reaffirmed her decision to avoid him for the rest of the journey. No good could come of encouraging the feelings she had for him, and that being the case it would be better if she did not see him at all.

To this end she decided to spend the day visiting the Turkish baths and the gymnasium. She longed to see them in their own right, but she also knew she would not see Carl there as men and women were given different times of usage. If she should, by chance, encounter him anywhere about the ship she would treat him with cool politeness. She was sure he would be horrified if he realized she had read anything into his attentions other than thanks for helping his mother, and she did not mean to disgrace herself by allowing him to guess that she had feelings for him.

She dressed quickly, slipping on her camisole, drawers and corset before putting a square-necked dress on top of them, then tidying her hair before going to the dining room for breakfast. A quick glance reassured her that Carl was not present. Having eaten her fill of poached eggs, scones, fruit and marmalade, she returned to her stateroom and composed her telegram to Charlie.

'Dear Charlie,

I am aboard *Titanic*. I will be arriving in New York on Wednesday. Can I see you? Emilia Cavendish.'

It was short and to the point. Anything more would have to wait until she saw him. She was about to make her way to the telegraph office when she hesitated. Barker was still at large on the ship, and it was possible he would try to kidnap her. However, he would be stopped by the stewards if he tried to enter the first-class part of the ship, she reassured herself, and even if he did, by some chance, slip through, he could not drag her all the way back to steerage without anyone seeing. Unsettling though it was to know that he was on board, she did not believe he could do her any harm until the ship reached New York.

Besides, she could not spend the rest of her voyage in her cabin just because of Barker. There was too much she wanted to see.

The telegraph office was busy, as usual, but she was assured her telegraph would be sent that morning. Then she embarked on the rest of her schedule.

The Turkish baths were in a part of the ship she had not yet visited, and she had to ask one of the stewards where she could find them. She was directed to the lower part of the ship. She had never had a Turkish bath and did not know quite what to expect, but the woman in charge explained it to her, telling her about the hot, temperate and cool rooms, and explaining the use of the massage couch and the plunge pool.

She undressed, wrapping herself in a towel, and went in. Like everything else on board *Titanic* the Turkish Baths were magnificent. The walls were made of enamelled tiles in rich shades of blue and green, whilst blue and white tiles covered the floor. Bronze lamps hung from the ceiling, which was supported by slender, intricately carved pillars. Couches upholstered in vibrant orange were arranged around the walls, and small tables were set in between them. She felt as though she had wandered into a scene from *Arabian Nights*.

She enjoyed the novel experience of the baths, falling into conversation with a number of other ladies who were enjoying themselves in the hot and steamy rooms. She decided to have a massage, and found it extremely relaxing, then went through to the plunge pool.

It was in the plunge pool she made the acquaintance of Mrs Pansy Wainfleet.

'Isn't this heavenly?' asked Mrs Wainfleet, as she relaxed in the cooling water.

'It's wonderful,' agreed Emilia.

'My name is Pansy, by the way, Pansy Wainfleet,' said Pansy, introducing herself.

Pansy was a few years older than Emilia, being in her late twenties. She had dark hair, dark eyes, and Emilia warmed to her straightaway.

'Emilia Cavendish,' said Emilia.

'I'm very pleased to meet you.'

Emilia did not find it surprising that Pansy had introduced herself without waiting for a mutual acquaintance to perform the ceremony. On board ship, it seemed, an informality prevailed that would have been unthinkable on dry land.

'Have you ever taken a Turkish bath before?' asked Pansy, as she stretched herself in the cooling water.

'No,' confessed Emilia. 'This is my first one.'

'Mine, too,' said Pansy. 'I never thought I would take a Turkish bath aboard a ship, but there is so much to do on *Titanic*. It's like no other ship I've ever been on. It offers so many opportunities, and all of them interesting and enjoyable.'

Emilia agreed.

'Have you been on a big ship before?' asked Pansy.

'Never,' confessed Emilia. 'This is my first time.'

'Robert and I cross the Atlantic regularly,' said Pansy. 'His business is in America, which is where we live, but we still have family in England and we like to visit them as often as possible. I couldn't believe it when he said we'd be returning on *Titanic*. We were meant to be travelling on *Philadelphia* but she was laid up because of the coal strike and so we transferred to *Titanic* instead. I'm so glad we did. I thought *Olympic* was wonderful, but she's nothing to *Titanic*.'

They compared their experiences of the ship and all the varied entertainments she offered her guests, soon falling into an easy friendship. Pansy was entertaining, and knew a great deal about the various ships belonging to the White Star Line, so that by the end of their bathe Emilia felt not only well entertained, but as though she had learnt many things as well.

At the end of their session in the Turkish baths, Pansy said, 'Would you join us for dinner tonight, Emilia? Robert and I are dying to try the à la carte restaurant. Dinner in the dining room is superb, but we want to sample everything *Titanic* has to offer, and the restaurant has a very good reputation. It's run by a Frenchman, you know, a Monsieur Gatti. He used to manage the restaurant of the Ritz. You'd be our guest, of course. Do say you'll come.'

Emilia was delighted with the idea. She had seen the restaurant on her way round the ship and had thought how splendid it looked. It would be wonderful to dine there, especially with a companion as entertaining as Pansy. Besides, by avoiding the dining room she would have an opportunity to avoid Carl Latimer, which was a very good thing. Mr Latimer was not proving easy to banish from her thoughts, and the less she saw of him the better.

'Thank you,' she said to Pansy. 'I'd love to. What time are you intending to dine?'

'Shall we say eight o'clock?'

'Eight o'clock. I'll look forward to it.'

The à la carte restaurant was in a beautiful room on the bridge deck. Emilia had thought she could not be surprised any more by the wonders of the ship, but she had been wrong. The restaurant was breathtaking. It was panelled from floor to ceiling in French walnut, and decorated with furniture in Louis-the-sixteenth style. Large bay windows gave an air of being in a country house, whilst their fawn curtains complemented the Axminster carpet, which was in a beautiful shade of *Rose du Barri*. At the after end was a bandstand raised on a platform, and musicians were playing. The lighting was discreet, and the atmosphere wonderful. Many of *Titanic*'s passengers were enjoying Monsieur Gatti's superb food, and the buzz of conversation filled the air.

Emilia met Pansy and Robert just outside. Pansy was beautifully dressed in a dark red Empire-line gown, with a feather in her hair. Robert, a handsome man with a jovial countenance, was dressed in smart evening attire. Pansy performed the introductions, and the three of them were shown to a splendid table at the front of the restaurant.

Once they had settled themselves they perused the menu, which contained a mouth-watering selection of dishes, and finally gave their order.

'Isn't this wonderful?' sighed Pansy. 'I've never seen so

many famous people in all my life. Look, over there by the door, just entering the restaurant, that's John Jacob Astor. They say Colonel Astor is one of the richest men in the world.'

'Really, Pansy,' said her husband, but without rancour. He was clearly used to Pansy's harmless enjoyment in spotting the rich and famous, and did no more than to offer a token remonstrance.

'The girl beside him is his new wife. Their marriage was quite a scandal,' went on Pansy, taking no notice of her husband and turning to Emilia. 'Madeleine is only eighteen years old – younger than his son. They went to Egypt right after the wedding, to avoid the gossip, but Madeleine's in a delicate condition so they're heading back to New York. And look, behind them, that's Margaret Brown. She comes from a family of Irish immigrants, and she married a miner. You wouldn't think so to look at her now, would you?'

'He made his fortune somehow or other,' Pansy went on, 'and she rose to become one of Denver's most prominent citizens. They don't see a lot of each other nowadays, though. He doesn't like the high life, and she does. She's been staying with the Astors in Cairo, but her grandchild's ill so she's going home.'

Pansy's eyes travelled round the room. 'Over there's Dickinson Bishop,' Pansy continued. 'He's from Michigan. He's been on honeymoon, too, with his second wife Helen. And at the next table is Paul Chevré the sculptor and Jacques Futrelle the writer – he writes mysteries, you know. Have you read any?'

'Yes, as a matter of fact, I have,' said Emilia.

She'd enjoyed Monsieur Futrelle's novels immensely, and was interested to see him in person. But she did not have long to look at him before Pansy pointed out the next celebrity.

'Over there's Henry B Harris, the Broadway producer. He's been over to London to see about a play for Rose Stahl, one of his actresses. And look, there's Archie Butt.'

'Major Butt,' her husband interposed.

'Very well, Major Butt,' said Pansy with the air of one humouring a child. 'He was military aide to President

Roosevelt, and then to President Taft, but his health's been suffering lately and he's been to Europe to recover.'

'A good thing, too,' said Robert. 'All that in-fighting must get a chap down.'

'Oh, politicians are always fighting,' said Pansy blithely. 'At the next table is Dorothy Gibson,' she said with a sigh. 'The lady with her is her mother. They are travelling together.' Emilia turned to look at Dorothy Gibson. Miss Gibson was a celebrated actress, and Emilia had seen one of her films with Aunt Clem.

'She's very beautiful,' she said.

And indeed Miss Gibson, with her fine features and expressive eyes, was very lovely.

'Isn't she?' sighed Pansy. 'I think she's even more beautiful in real life than she is on the screen. I'd love to go and talk to her, but I can't pluck up the courage to do so. She's just made a new film, I hear, called *The Easter Bonnet*. I'm dying to ask her all about it, but I don't suppose I'll get the chance.'

Emilia was enjoying herself immensely. Pansy recognized a great many people, and Emilia was learning a lot about her fellow passengers. It was almost worth missing her chance to disembark at Queenstown, just to see so many famous faces.

It was also a help in diverting her thoughts from Carl. She had hoped that by dining in the à la carte restaurant, where she would not see him, her thoughts would not keep straying to him, but she had been wrong. Memories of the evening before kept returning to her. She couldn't stop herself recalling the way he looked, the things he'd said, and the way he'd smiled. Even with Pansy's conversation sparkling round her she could not stop thinking about him; without it, she would have thought of nothing else.

Emilia could hardly believe she had been on *Titanic* for almost three days. So much had happened, and the time had passed so quickly. But as she wrote up her account of the voyage on the morning following her meal with Pansy, the morning of

Saturday 13th April, she realized just how long she had been at sea.

The weather had been beautiful, and this morning was no exception. Having finished her writing, she decided to take a turn on the deck. She donned her coat, gloves and hat, then went out into the fresh air.

A number of early risers were already there, admiring the ocean. It stretched out in an unbroken vista in every direction, looking calm and placid beneath the clear sky.

Further along the deck, a game of quoits was going on, and past that a couple were playing deck golf. In sheltered nooks and crannies out of the wind, people were sitting in deckchairs supplied for their enjoyment, and stewards were carrying trays of refreshments to and fro.

As she stood there, watching the ocean, two crew members walked past her, talking.

'I still don't like this ship,' said one. 'I have a queer feeling about it.'

'Come on,' said his companion. 'She's a wonderful ship.'

'I don't know so much. I'm not the only one to have a queer feeling about her. Arthur Lewis, one of the stewards, is anxious as well. His wife put his White Star in his cap the night before we sailed, and it fell to pieces in her hands. "I don't like this," she said, and I'm not surprised. Arthur didn't like it above half, either.'

'Superstition,' said the other crewman, but all the same he sounded a little less sure of himself.

'John Stewart's not happy,' the first crewman continued.

'The verandah café steward?'

'Yes. His wife saw him off at Southampton. It's unlucky. Wives should never see their husbands off. He's convinced something's going to happen.'

'To him, maybe, but not the whole ship. Perhaps he's going to trip over his own feet!'

But despite his nervous attempt at a joke, the mood did not lighten.

'And then there's Joseph Scarrott. He said "goodbye" to his sister, and not "so long, see you again soon" as he always does. And now one of the passengers, a hard-headed man, a New York lawyer, Isaac Frauenthal, had a dream before we set sail. He was on a ship, it crashed into something and started to go down. He could hear the shouts of people drowning.'

'Better stop this. You're starting to make me worry now,' said the other crewman. 'In fact, you're starting to make me wish I'd followed Coffy's example and jumped ship.'

'The fireman?'

'That's right. One of the boiler stokers. He hid under the mail sacks going ashore and got off at Queenstown. Never got back on again.' He gave a nervous laugh. 'You don't suppose he'd had a premonition, too, do you?'

'Who knows?'

They passed out of hearing.

It was only idle superstition, Emilia reassured herself as she looked out over the calm blue waters. It seemed impossible to think of any disaster befalling *Titanic*, with the spring sunshine glimmering on the quiet sea. Even so, she felt less comfortable than she had done ten minutes before.

'Is something worrying you?'

She heard the familiar voice at her elbow and turned to see Carl approaching her. He was dressed in an overcoat and gloves, with a bowler hat. He looked very smart, but not even the superb cut of his clothes could hide the fact that he was a vibrant man with a ruthless streak, rather than the sophisticated gentleman he appeared.

She felt her heart start to beat more quickly as he gave her a brilliant smile. It was all very well for her to tell herself that she must not find him attractive. Unfortunately, she did. His face was strong, giving evidence of his character, and she could not help remembering how it had felt to be held in his arms. She had better not think of it. If she did, she would give herself away.

'Mr Latimer,' she said as coolly as she could.

'Miss Cavendish. I'm glad to see you again.' He came to a stop a few feet in front of her, rested the tip of his cane on the deck, then folded his hands on its top. 'You left the dining room very quickly the other night. I hope you were not too unwell?'

'No, it was nothing. Just a little sickness, that's all,' she said.

She did not know why, but she had a feeling he did not believe she had been unwell. But she could not tell him the truth; that she had been distressed to learn of his forthcoming engagement.

'I hope you're feeling all right now?'

'Yes, thank you. I have quite recovered.'

'Good. I'm glad. Sea sickness can be very unpleasant. Even on a ship like this it's impossible to completely avoid it.' He glanced out over the calm water. 'There might not be any motion caused by the waves, but there is always the throb of the engines.'

'That is so.'

The wind had risen, and although her hat was held on with a pin, she did not trust it and put her hand on her hat to stop it blowing away.

'But if you are feeling better then ill health can't be the cause of the worried expression you were wearing just now. So what caused it?'

He looked at her searchingly.

'It's nothing,' she said.

He waited.

She tried to keep it in, but at last her feelings got the better of her.

'Mr Latimer, just how safe is this ship?' she burst out.

He eyed her thoughtfully. 'Has something happened to make you concerned?' he asked.

'No, not really. It's just that I heard some of the crewmen talking. One was saying he didn't like the ship, and that he's not the only one. A number of crew members have had presentiments of disaster.'

'Sailors always have presentiments of disaster,' he said reassuringly, 'but they very rarely come true. If they did, every ship ever built would end up on the bottom of the sea.'

She gave a rueful smile. 'I'm sure you're right. Even so, just how safe is *Titanic*?'

'She's probably the safest ship ever built.'

'So if there was an accident, she wouldn't sink?' she asked, holding on to her hat more tightly. The wind had become even stronger, and it whipped her coat around her ankles as well as trying to pull the hat from her head.

'It's very unlikely. She has some of the most up-to-date safety features ever devised. I was talking to Andrews about it only yesterday. She has a double hull, and a series of water-tight bulkheads down below that will protect her if she should, by any chance, hit something. Say she'd hit the small vessel that broke its moorings when we were leaving Southampton, and say the collision had punched a hole in her, she would still have been able to float.'

'I don't understand,' said Emilia with a frown. 'I don't know what you mean by bulkheads.'

'They're like walls, dividing the lower part of the ship into sixteen separate compartments,' he explained. 'That way, if the hull's ruptured, only one of the compartments will flood and the water will be kept out of the rest of the ship.'

'So the compartments are like boxes?' she asked.

'Yes, but without a lid.'

'Without a lid? But if they don't have a lid, what's to stop the water from getting into one compartment and then going over the top of the bulkhead into the next one?'

'In theory, nothing. But the ship would have to be taking on a lot of water for that to happen. The bulkheads reach ten feet above the waterline.'

'But if one of them's flooded, as long as water doesn't spill over the top into the next one, the ship can still float?'

'Yes And not just with one compartment flooded, but with two compartments flooded, or four of the smaller bow compartments. So you see, even if we do hit something, there's almost no chance the ship will sink.'

Emilia breathed a sigh of relief.

'Did you believe in the superstitions?' he asked her curiously.

'Not exactly. But it did make me think. If anything happened to us out here, we'd be a long way from help.'

She looked out over the ocean.

'We're not as far away from help as you think,' he said. 'Ships use these routes all the time. Besides, it would be easy to signal them using the Marconi wireless system if there was a need. And as a last resort there are always the lifeboats.'

She glanced at the wooden boats hanging from the davits. They were covered over, and looked very clean and smart. There were sixteen of them in all, eight on the port side of the ship, where she and Carl now stood, and a matching eight on the starboard side of the ship. They were very sturdy, but they did not look large enough to carry everyone on board.

'How many people does *Titanic* carry?' she asked, as she walked over to one of the lifeboats and tried to estimate how many people could sit inside.

'Over three thousand when she's full. There are just over two thousand people on board at the moment. The coal strike in England put a lot of people off travelling, as they didn't think the voyage would go ahead. Why do you ask?'

'Just looking at these boats, it seems to me they would not take more than fifty or sixty people each. With sixteen boats, that's not enough room for a thousand people. Even if I'm wrong about how many people can fit in each one, there still can't be enough room for over two thousand.'

He eyed them thoughtfully. 'You could have a point. There are a few collapsible boats on board as well, but I believe there are only four of them. There don't seem to be enough boats to save everyone if the ship should sink. I know Andrews wanted to put double the number of lifeboats on board. He used strong davits on purpose. They will take two lifeboats each, instead of only one.'

'Then why didn't he?' asked Emilia, pushing her hair back from her face as the wind whipped stray tendrils loose from her chignon.

'He was overruled. It was thought a double row of lifeboats would make the deck look too cluttered.'

Emilia looked along the length of the deck. It was true that the lifeboats took up a lot of room, occupying perhaps half the width of the deck in some places. It was also true that, being taller than a man when they were strung up on the davits at the side of the deck, they reduced the view of the sea.

'There would certainly be less space for walking,' agreed Emilia. 'Even so . . .'

'I agree. It's safety that's important aboard a ship, not appearances. Still, I shouldn't worry about it. We'll be in New York by Wednesday, and then you won't have to think about it any more.'

She looked out over the ocean, breathing in the salty tang of the sea air. There was nothing but water in every direction. But in a few more days they would see land once again.

She smiled. 'I expect you think I'm foolish.'

'Not at all. *Titanic*'s a marvel, but it doesn't do to forget that she's made of iron, and that anything made of iron can sink. Prudence as well as an eye for beauty is needed when designing a ship.'

The wind intensified, and a sudden gust blew across the deck, pulling her hat from her head. She tried to grasp it, but it was whipped out of her reach.

Carl stretched out his hand and caught it.

'Thank you,' she said.

She held out her hand.

Instead of giving it back to her, however, he tucked his cane under his arm.

'Here, let me help you,' he said.

As his deft fingers ran through her hair, she stilled. The feel of his fingers in her golden locks was mesmerizing. Her scalp began to tingle. She was filled with an almost irresistible urge to turn her head so that his fingers would run over the crown of her head, but she forced herself to resist it. She must not betray, by word or deed, the effect he was having on her. But even though she said nothing, even though she did not move, she thought he sensed it.

His fingers stilled.

She stopped breathing.

Then she felt his hands running over her forehead before tracing the line of her cheek. His touch was gossamer light and made her shiver. She marvelled that such strong hands could be so delicate. With such strange and unnerving, yet delightful, sensations coursing through her she did not dare to look at him. If she did, she was sure he would see her feelings written all over her face. His fingers stroked down the line of her cheek and came to rest beneath her chin.

She swallowed. And then what she had dreaded happened. He lifted her chin, so that she was forced to look at him. She tried to hide her feelings, but they would not be disguised. She felt her eyes opening wide as she drank him in. She saw his own eyes flash in response, and for one insane moment she thought he was going to kiss her. There was a look on his face that told her the idea was in his mind, as well as in hers.

She couldn't understand why she should want him to do it. It was not as though she liked being kissed. It was terrible. Mr Montmorency had kissed her, and it had been dreadful. But the thought of Carl kissing her was somehow enticing. How would it feel? she wondered. Would it be hard and powerful, as he himself was hard and powerful? Or would it be tender?

She must put a stop to this, she realized with a gulp. She was letting her feelings run away with her. They were on the boat deck, in a public place, and although for the moment the deck was empty, at any moment it could become busy again.

'Can . . .' Her word came out breathlessly. She took a hold on herself. 'Can you not find the pin?' she asked.

'Yes. I can find it,' he said.

He made no move to take it out, however, but continued to hold her with his gaze.

'Then . . .' She swallowed. 'Won't you pull it out?'

There was a long moment. She thought it would never end. She was not sure she wanted it to end. But then, to her relief – and also her inexpressible disappointment – his fingers returned to her hair, and she felt the pin glide over her scalp. As he pulled it out, several tendrils of hair were pulled loose with it.

His fingers moved deftly in reaction, combing her hair back from her face, and she felt as though she had escaped from one danger only to fall into another. The feel of them as they ran through her hair was intoxicating. She stood quite still whilst he fastened the loose strands, pushing them back into her chignon.

His hands lingered for a moment longer than necessary. Then, taking her hat from beneath his arm, he pinned it back on to her head.

'Thank you,' she said, not meeting his eye.

'Don't mention it.'

He turned to look along the deck.

Without his eyes on her, she felt her pulse begin to calm.

'Would you like to take a walk?' he asked.

She hesitated. She should not spend any more time in his company than was necessary, but she could think of no reason to refuse without being rude.

'Very well.'

He offered her his arm. She rested her fingers on it so lightly that they could barely feel the muscles beneath his coat.

They turned and walked along the deck, towards the stern of the ship.

'Have you been enjoying your extra time on *Titanic*?' he asked.

'Yes, very much so,' she said, relieved to be on safe ground. 'I went to the Turkish baths yesterday, and then spent a while in the gymnasium.'

'That explains why I didn't see you. You weren't at dinner,' he remarked.

'I dined in the à la carte restaurant, with Pansy Wainfleet and her husband. I met Pansy in the baths,' she explained.

'Ah. I see.'

They walked on, past a little boy playing with a whip and top. He had chalked on the top, creating a colourful pattern which merged into a blur as the top spun across the deck.

'I am hoping to experience everything *Titanic* has to offer before we reach New York,' she said.

'What will you do when we get there?' he asked. 'Will you put up at a hotel until you can arrange for your return passage?'

'A hotel, or a lodging house.'

'And do you intend to see the sights?'

'I do. I have a friend living over there who sells antiques, and I am hoping he will show me round.'

'Have you telegraphed to let him know you're coming?'

'Yes. I did so as soon as I thought of it. I haven't had a reply yet, but I think he will be pleased to see me.'

'Ah.' he hesitated. 'He is someone special?' he asked. His tone was superficially light, but there was an edge to his voice, and a tenseness about him that told her he was keeping himself in check. For some reason the idea that Charlie might be special bothered him.

'Yes. He is a very dear friend of mine. I've know Charlie since we were children,' she replied.

'I see. Then he is not your fiancé?'

His question startled her, and also flustered her. 'I hardly think that's any of your business,' she replied.

'It might not be any of my business, but I'm curious.' He stopped and turned to look at her. His eyes traced the lines of her face. 'You're a beautiful young woman, Emilia, and yet you're not married. You've known poverty, but you've also known something better. Have you never been tempted to marry in order to get back what you lost?'

The idea brought back vivid memories. Bad memories.

'No. Never,' she said vehemently, taking her hand from his arm.

He looked at her curiously.

'To marry to escape poverty,' she continued. 'It isn't worth — ' She broke off suddenly.

'It isn't worth what?' he asked.

'Nothing,' she said, biting her tongue.

'You were intrigued by me. When we danced at dinner, I satisfied your curiosity. Won't you satisfy mine?'

There was an intensity to his gaze that unsettled her. His questions seemed prompted by more than idle curiosity. It was as though he wanted to get to know her, and find out what events had shaped her personality. The idea made her afraid. It was too intimate. If she told him too much about herself she would find it very difficult not to draw close to him. And that would be unwise.

'There's really nothing to tell,' she said.

She looked out over the sea. As her eyes returned to the deck, she caught sight of something that made her shiver. It was a figure on the third-class poop deck.

Barker. He had only to turn round and he would see her.

'You're cold,' said Carl, seeing her shiver. 'We'll go in. Will you join me in the café for a cup of coffee?'

'No. I'm sorry, I can't,' she said hastily, turning her back towards the poop deck in an effort to escape Barker's notice. 'I have an appointment,' she said, thinking quickly. She must go below before Barker saw her, no matter how rude she appeared. 'I arranged to meet Pansy. I've only just remembered. Please excuse me. I must go.'

And then before he could try and stop her she hurried away, back along the deck and down the stairs. Seeing Barker had reawakened all her fears. For the time being she was safe enough – if he wandered into first-class accommodation he would be stopped by the stewards, and there was no danger of him abducting her in third-class as she had no intention of venturing into steerage again – but once they neared New York she would no longer be safe. With all the bustle of disembarkation, it would be easy for Barker to strike.

Even worse, she could not think what to do about it.

Below deck, in a sumptuous first-class stateroom, Mrs Gisborne was reclining on a damask-upholstered sofa.

'Damn it, where's that magazine?' said her husband, as he looked through a pile of newspapers and magazines on the console table. 'You know the one I mean, Margaret. The one with the article about the stud.'

Mrs Gisborne shifted slightly but did not reply.

'It was here on Thursday. This is ridiculous, where can it have got to?' He called out to the maid. 'Janice . . . Janice?'.

'If you are going to ask Janice where it is you needn't bother,' said his wife, idly turning the pages of her book. 'It isn't here. I . . . lent it to someone.'

'Well you can just unlend it,' he said. 'There was an article on Hugo's stud I wanted to read.'

'You can't have it,' she said.

His eyes sharpened. 'Why can't I? What do you mean?'

'I mean I gave it to Miss Cavendish, and I am not about to ask for it back.'

'Miss Cavendish? What the devil would Miss Cavendish want with . . . Ah. The picture of Carl and Isabelle.'

His wife sat up and put her book aside. 'There's no use letting the poor girl encourage unfortunate feelings for him,' she said. 'I wanted to put her on her guard.'

'Wanted to scare her off, you mean,' he grumbled.

'And you don't?' she demanded. 'You would like to see Isabelle reduced to rags?'

'No . . . well . . .' he blustered.

'Because that's what she will be, if Latimer doesn't come up to scratch. My poor sister's been penniless since Paul died. She thought he'd leave her well provided for, but instead he left her nothing but debts. A good marriage for Isabelle is the only thing that can save them both from the poorhouse, and I'm not about to let a jumped up little nobody take him away from her.'

'It seems a bit rough on Latimer,' said Thomas, pursing his lips.

'I don't see why. Carl Latimer is a dear boy, and he is delighted to be marrying into such a well-connected family,' she returned. 'And why shouldn't he be? Isabelle's beautiful, charming and elegant. Together they'll have fine children.'

'Carl Latimer's no boy, and if you ask me, this idea you've got of making a pet of him won't work out. He might be marrying Isabelle for her connections, but you'd do well to tread warily until the ring's on her finger. There are plenty of other hard-up young women with good families who'd love to have such a fine looking man in the family, especially one who happens to be a millionaire.'

A frown crossed her exquisitely made-up face.

'You could be right. The Pargeters have been chasing him. So have the Theakstons. The sooner Isabelle fixes his interest the better.' She paused momentarily. 'It would be a good idea if Susan and Isabelle came to meet him when the ship docks in New York. Perhaps they'd better make it look like an accident – in fact, they can pretend they are meeting me. If Isabelle is there at the pier, looking elegant and glamorous, it will remind him just how inferior Miss Cavendish is. She's all very well for a shipboard romance, but when it comes to the serious business of marriage, the sight of Isabelle should remind him that only a well-bred and well-connected wife will do. I'll telegraph Susan straightaway and let her know.'

Mr Gisborne picked up a newspaper. 'If you say so. But I still think Latimer will slip the net.'

'Oh, no,' said Mrs Gisborne calmly. 'Depend upon it. Between us, Susan, Isabelle and I will make sure he comes up to scratch.'

Six

Emilia had arranged to meet Pansy and Robert for lunch, and at twelve o'clock she joined them in the dining room. They seated themselves at a table next to one of the leaded-light windows overlooking the ocean.

'I'm starving,' said Pansy, she picked up the menu. 'Robert and I were up early. I have already been for a walk along the deck and a swim this morning. I could eat a horse!'

'It looks like horse is the one thing that isn't on the menu,' joked Robert.

Emilia's eye ran down the mouth-watering dishes on offer.

There was a choice of soup, with fish to follow, and there was a selection from the grill. As if this wasn't enough, there was also a buffet, with salmon, shrimps, herrings, sardines, roast meats, pies, hams, sausages and salads. Afterwards, a tempting selection of cheeses vied with a choice of pastries. She would need another walk after lunch!

Having made their selection, they ordered what they wanted and exchanged news of their morning. Emilia, however, found it hard to concentrate on what Pansy was saying. The sight of Barker had reminded her of her danger and made her anxious, and she found herself worrying about what would happen when the ship neared New York. Would he try and kidnap her whilst she was still on the ship? She thought not. He would be more likely to do it once the ship had docked.

'Tell me,' she said, when Pansy had finished telling her about the swimming pool. 'What happens when we disembark?'

'We get off at one of the piers,' said Pansy. 'It's much like embarkation, except we walk down the gangplank instead of up it.'

'Do the different classes of accommodation disembark separately?' she asked casually.

'Oh, yes. They have their own gangplanks,' she said.

'And at customs?' she asked. 'What happens then? Do first-class passengers go through separately, or do they mingle with people from steerage?'

Pansy looked curious. 'Do you know, I'd never really thought about it. Do we see anyone from steerage when we go through customs?' Pansy asked Robert.

Robert was busy sipping Munich lager beer.

'I'm not sure,' he said. 'I don't think so, but I've never noticed. Don't worry,' he continued, smiling reassuringly at Emilia, 'people in steerage are really not that bad, you know. They're mostly clean, and some of them are quite decent. It's always as well to hold on to your possessions, of course. There's no point in putting temptation in people's way. But you've nothing to fear from them.'

Realizing they had misunderstood her interest, she thought of telling them what it was that was troubling her, but she did not want to burden them with her problems. Besides, she did not think they would be able to help her. Charming though Pansy and Robert were, she could not imagine them knowing how to deal with someone like Barker.

But Carl would know how to deal with him. It was an unwelcome thought, but she could not deny the truth of it. He was used to mixing with people from all walks of life, and on his way up from poverty he must have had many difficult situations to deal with. If only she could ask him about it, she felt sure he would be able to advise her on what precautions she should take against being abducted.

However, she had no intention of asking him. In order to explain the situation she would have to tell him about herself, and she was not ready to do so. It would involve them in further intimacy, and she was already growing too close to him. She must not allow herself to grow any closer.

Her distraction, fortunately, had gone unnoticed. Pansy was

in fine form, regaling her with stories about the card sharps who had boarded the ship with the hope of fleecing the wealthy passengers.

'Do you see that man sitting over there?' she asked, indicating a man sitting by himself at a nearby table. 'That's Tom McAuliffe. He's part of a band of card sharps on the ship. He's well known to the police.'

'Really, Pansy, I don't think this is a suitable subject for conversation over lunch,' said her husband reprovingly.

'Why not?' rejoined his wife, not at all put out.

'I hardly think Emilia needs to know about men like that. It's not as though she's likely to be fleeced by professional gamblers,' joked Robert.

They laughed.

'You never know,' teased Pansy. 'Perhaps she has a secret vice. Or perhaps,' she said, turning to her husband mischievously, 'I meant it as a warning for you.'

'My dear wife, you are a little minx,' he teased her back affectionately. 'I have many faults, but gambling isn't one of them.'

'What are your plans for this afternoon?' asked Emilia, as the waiter brought their dessert. It was a wonderful pastry concoction, and the sight of it made her mouth water.

'I was going to write some postcards, and then we were going to play bridge in the lounge, but after this I think I will need to spend a session in the gymnasium!' said Pansy, her eyes growing wide.

'I know what you mean,' smiled Emilia. 'It is a good thing there are so many things to do on *Titanic,* otherwise, with all the food on board, there would be a lot of gowns that no longer fitted!'

'Do you play bridge, Emilia?' asked Robert, as he contented himself with a piece of cheese. 'Perhaps you would care to join us.'

'That's very kind,' said Emilia, 'but I want to continue exploring the ship.'

'But you'll be at divine service in the morning, won't you?' asked Pansy, through a mouthful of pastry.

'Yes. I'm looking forward to it.'

'Good. We'll see you there. And after divine service there'll be the lifeboat drill. There's always a lifeboat drill on the first Sunday of a voyage.'

'That should be interesting,' said Emilia, thinking she would have an opportunity to find out more about the small wooden boats that lined the deck, and how they would operate in case of an emergency.

Their meal came to an end. Arranging to meet the following morning, they went their separate ways. Pansy and Robert went into the lounge, and Emilia made her way to the reading room.

Alone again, Emilia's thought returned to Barker. Whilst listening to Pansy's lively chatter she had had some distraction from her thoughts, but now they returned with full force. What if Barker tried to kidnap her when she left the ship at New York? What should she do? For if he managed it, he would turn her over to Mr Silas Montmorency, and the thought made her shudder.

She was still worrying about it as she entered the reading room. She scarcely noticed its high ceiling, white panelling and gold-upholstered chairs, splendid though they were. She stopped suddenly as something finally penetrated her thoughts. For there, sitting on one of the gold sofas, reading a newspaper, was Carl Latimer. Even worse, there was no one else in the room. She was about to back out quietly and close the door when he looked up and saw her.

He stood up. 'Miss Cavendish,' he said.

'Mr Latimer. I'm sorry. I didn't mean to disturb you.'

'You're not disturbing me.' He smiled. 'Please, stay.'

She hesitated, then said, 'Very well.'

She did not join him, however. Instead she crossed to the far side of the room and sat down at one of the tables by the window. There were some newspapers lying about and she picked one up, trying to take an interest in its articles, but her thoughts wandered and she found herself looking out to sea instead. It was so calm and placid; it was the complete opposite of her thoughts. She turned her attention back to the

newspaper, but her mind was not on what she was reading.
'Mr Latimer?' she said at last.

He looked up from his newspaper.

She lay her own down on the table. 'Mr Latimer,' she began again.

'Would it really be too dreadful for you to call me Carl?' he asked, folding his newspaper and dropping it on the sofa before walking over to join her.

Feeling she would be at a disadvantage if she remained seated, she stood up. 'Yes, I'm afraid it would,' she said, as he joined her by the window.

She was already regretting her decision to ask for his help. He was so close to her that he was clouding her senses, and she felt that if she was sensible she would get away from him as quickly as possible. But it would not only be bad manners, if she did so, it would look decidedly odd. So she must stay. But as for calling him by his first name, it was out of the question. Unfortunately, he was not prepared to let the matter drop.

'Why?' he asked.

'Why?' She was taken aback. 'I would have thought that was obvious. It would be most improper.'

He shrugged. 'I know most people would think so, but frankly, I'm not interested in what most people think. I'm interested in what you think. So if you think it's impossible, I'd like to know why.'

There was something challenging about him.

'Really,' she said, turning away from him and walking across the room to the mantelpiece. 'I hardly know you . . .'

'So you will call me Carl when you do?' he asked.

He followed her with his eyes, but he did not close the distance between them, letting her escape. Even so, she was aware of his presence. Although he was at the other side of the room, he still seemed very near.

'Mr Latimer,' she said, fast feeling she was losing control of the situation, and speaking with as much dignity as she could muster, 'Given that we are simply shipmates, it is impossible that I should get to know you better. When the ship docks, you will go your way and I will go mine.'

'There you go with that word again. Impossible.' He smiled, and it brought his eyes to life. 'It seems to me that nothing in life is truly impossible.'

She turned towards the mantelpiece and straightened the clock. 'Not for you, perhaps.'

She caught sight of his frown in the mirror.

'Something's troubling you,' he said. The bantering note had gone from his voice and he was suddenly serious.

She hesitated. She wanted his help, needed his help. But even so . . . And yet, she must have some advice. She took a deep breath and decided to take the plunge, because if Barker was able to take hold of her when the ship docked she could well find herself kidnapped.

'What is it?' he asked her gently. 'What's wrong?'

It was strange that his voice could be so gentle. Caressing, even.

'It's nothing . . .' she began.

He waited.

'It's just that . . .' She spun round to look at him. 'Mr Latimer, you have sailed before. I was just wondering, what happens when we leave the ship?'

He looked surprised, but nevertheless he answered her question, telling her about the procedure for disembarking and going through customs.

'Are the classes kept separate on leaving the ship?' she said, asking him the question she had asked Pansy. It was of such importance that she needed to be certain.

'Yes. They are. Why?'

'Oh, nothing.' She was not yet ready to confide in him entirely. 'I just wondered, that's all. Are there any places . . . is there anywhere the different classes come into contact?'

He eyed her curiously. Then said,' Why don't you tell me what it is that's troubling you?'

'There's nothing,' she said brightly. 'I was just curious, that's all.'

'No. It's more than that. You're worried about something – and don't tell me it's about disembarkation, because I don't

believe you. Has someone in steerage been bothering you?'
She hesitated again, wondering how much she should say.

'Something frightened you on Thursday,' he said, walking towards her and stopping a few feet in front of her. He looked down at her in concern. 'It frightened you so badly that you ran across the deck and into my arms. You were in steerage at the time. Now you are asking me if you will have to meet anyone from steerage when you disembark. What is it, Emilia? What happened? And why are you frightened it might happen again?'

She bit her lip.

'Won't you trust me?' he asked softly. 'If you do, I might be able to help you.'

She looked at him, trying to make up her mind. He was a wealthy man, ruthless and hard. And yet she had the innate feeling that he was trustworthy. He might be like Silas Montmorency in circumstances, but he was nothing like him in character. And it was character that determined a man's actions, not his wealth.

'Very well.' She paused, then began. 'There is a man by the name of Barker. I knew him in Southampton. Two days ago, I saw him on the ship.' She paused again. 'He is in the employ of a gentleman named Silas Montmorency.'

He said nothing, but waited for her to continue.

She walked over to the window and looked over the sea. 'When I was younger, I lived in the Cotswolds, but when I was nineteen my parents were killed in an accident and I went to live in Southampton with my Aunt Clem. She was a wonderful woman. She was always cheerful, and so full of life. She took me in and looked after me, and although her circumstances were straitened, she did everything in her power to cheer me and make me happy. I had always liked her, but the more I knew her, the more I came to love her. We lived very happily together, enjoying each other's company, until . . . until her death last year.'

She turned to face him. Her hands were clasped.

'Aunt Clem lived in a rented house. Once a month her land-lord would call to collect the rent. He was a respectable man, but he had a friend ... One day, this friend, Mr Silas Montmorency, accompanied the landlord to our house. He ... took a liking to me.'

Carl's mouth set in a grim line. 'I see.'

'Aunt Clem had taken the landlord out into the garden to show him her new bed of flowers. She loved flowers,' she said with a smile. Then her face darkened. 'Mr Montmorency ... he put his arms round me and he kissed me.' Her head dropped, and she shuddered with the memory of it. At length she roused herself. 'Whilst he was still embracing me, Aunt Clem came in. She was horrified. He told her that he meant no offence, and said that he wanted to marry me. He said he could give me everything I had lost. He sounded generous ... kindly ... but there was something about him that made me afraid. When he had pulled me into his arms, he had ignored my struggles and my repeated requests that he let me go. And when he had kissed me, he had made my skin crawl. He was a respectable man on the outside, but there was something poisonous about him underneath. It made me afraid of ever falling into his power. When I refused him, he became angry: he was a wealthy man, and he was used to getting his own way.'

'Ah.'

She could tell by his expression that he understood why she had been so hostile to him at their first meeting.

'He told me I could have six weeks to think about it, but that one way or another he would have me, either with a ring on my finger, or without.' She smoothed her skirt. 'Aunt Clem had been ill. Her health deteriorated rapidly. It was winter, and she fell ill with pneumonia. In her weakened state she did not live very long.' She bit her lip, for she had loved her Aunt Clem dearly. 'After the funeral, I moved to another lodging house. I thought I had shaken Mr Montmorency, but two months later I saw one of his henchmen following me home from the shops. He noted the house and then left. I knew he had gone to tell Mr Montmorency where I could be found. I didn't wait for him to return. I packed my bags and left at once. And so I have lived for the last few months, changing houses every time he found me. But I knew I could not do that forever. I thought of telling my godmother, but her husband had been ill and I did not want to worry her further. Her husband has made a good recovery, however, and she has invited me to live with them in Ireland. A friend of hers had booked passage on *Titanic* – they were friends in their schooldays, and Charlotte married very well. When Charlotte knew she would not be using her stateroom, as circumstances forced her into taking an earlier sailing to America, she wrote to my godmother and asked if she could make use of it. My godmother did not want to travel as she had just invited me to stay, but she knew I would be able to make use of it . . . and the rest you know.'

They fell silent. Outside the window, the Atlantic rolled majestically past.

At last he spoke. 'Some of the rest I know,' he said. 'but I don't know how Barker found you.'

'He saw me boarding the ship. He and Mr Montmorency had found me at my new lodgings, and I escaped just in time. They followed me from the house, looking for me. I thought I'd escaped them but Barker caught sight of me as I walked up the gangplank. He killed one of the steerage passengers for his ticket and followed me aboard. He could do nothing to begin with, because I was in first-class accommodation and he was in third, but when I went to look for the swimming pool and lost my way, I unwittingly played into his hands.'

'And that's why you missed your port?'

'Yes. He saw me. I ran, but he followed me. I lost my way in the maze of corridors. I finally managed to get on to the deck, but he was there already. I ran again, but found myself up against the railings. When he advanced on me I slipped past him and ran into you.' She raised her face and looked him in the eyes. 'If you had not been there . . .'

'But I was.' He took her hands in his own, and there was a moment of deep connection between them.

She felt herself relax. She knew she could trust him. 'I don't know what to do,' she said.

He pressed her hands reassuringly. 'Leave it to me. I'll

have my man keep an eye on him and make sure he remains in steerage for the rest of the voyage. And I will personally escort you from the ship.'

She felt a huge sense of relief. She was glad she had told him.

He lifted his hand, and for a moment she thought he was going to run the back of it across her cheek. But then he dropped it again, making her both relieved and strangely disappointed.

'But I'm concerned about what might happen to you in New York. It's possible Barker has telegraphed to Silas Montmorency, to let him know you will be there. And even if he hasn't, Barker himself is likely to pursue you. This friend of yours, the one you are meeting – will he be able to protect you?'

She hesitated. Charlie was a dear, but able to protect her? No.

'Because if he can't, I can.'

She knew that what he said was true. He was a strong man, and a determined one. He would be able to protect her from any danger that threatened her.

'That is very kind, but . . .'

'Would you consider staying with my mother and myself in New York, instead of your friend, until you can book a passage to Ireland? That way I could be sure you'd be safe.'

She was touched by his concern. 'That's very kind of you, but I don't think it would be proper.'

'With my mother there? It couldn't be anything else. I don't want to press you, but will you at least think about it?'

'Yes. Thank you. I will.'

A warm smile lit his eyes. It seemed as though he wanted her to stay. But then, he was just being kind, she reminded herself.

'Emilia,' he said, reaching out and clasping her hand.

The door opened, and the Countess of Rothes entered the room with her companion.

'Thank you,' said Emilia formally, hastily reclaiming her hand. 'You have been most kind.'

With the Countess there, he could say nothing to detain her, and she left the room. Her feelings were in turmoil. She longed to accept his offer, but she could not disguise from herself the fact that it had less to do with a desire to be safe than a desire to be with Carl. He drew her in a way no man had ever drawn her before. And yet she must not allow herself to indulge in such thoughts. His offer had sprung out of a concern for her safety and she would be foolish if she allowed herself to imagine it had been anything else.

Dangerous though it would be to stay in New York with Barker and Silas Montmorency looking for her, she had the unsettling feeling it would be far more dangerous, to her feelings at least, to stay with Carl Latimer.

Carl remained in the reading room only long enough to engage in a little polite conversation with the Countess of Rothes before he made his way down to second class to speak to Hutton. He knocked on the door of Hutton's room and was quickly admitted.

'There's something I want you to do,' he said, as Hutton hastily put on his coat. 'There's a man in steerage who goes by the name of Barker. I want him watched. On no account are you to let him pass through into first-class accommodation.'

'What do you want me to do if he tries it?' asked Hutton. 'Do you want me to come and tell you, or do you want me to stop him?'

'I want you to stop him. Use an excuse if you can, but if needs be use force.'

Hutton nodded.

'And Hutton, under no circumstances allow him to go near the telegraph office.'

'Very good, sir. How long am I to keep him under surveillance?'

'Until we leave the ship at New York. Possibly beyond. I'll let you know that at the time.'

'Very good, sir, I'll get right on it.'

'Good man.'

Carl left the room, and made his way to the telegraph office, intending to find out if Barker had sent a telegraph to Silas Montmerency, telling him that Emilia was aboard the ship. If that was the case, Carl needed to know about it, so that he could take additional steps to protect her in New York. The telegraph office was busy, but at last he was able to find that no telegrams had been sent to a Mr Montmorency. Barker wanted to be sure of her first, Carl guessed. No use saying he had her, and then leaving Monmorency to rave if he lost her. It was a relief, because protecting Emilia would have been a lot more difficult in New York, particularly if she had refused to stay with him.

He found his thoughts going to the man she intended to stay with. Who was he, this man? A childhood friend, she had said, but childhood friends could, on occasion, turn into something more.

At the thought of it he felt the stirrings of an uncomfortable emotion, and he realized it was jealousy. The strength of his feelings took him by surprise. He had never felt jealous of any man before, but couldn't hide from himself that fact that he was jealous of this Charlie. It was Charlie who would have the pleasure of Emilia's company in New York; Charlie who would have an opportunity to show her round the splendid city and take her to see the sights.

He gritted his teeth as he thought of it. One way or another, Emilia Cavendish seemed to have been created to destroy his peace of mind.

Seven

The weather became colder overnight. When Emilia ventured out on deck on Sunday morning she was glad of her warm coat, her gloves and her hat, because where the air touched her face it had a raw feel to it. It was not to be wondered at. They were now in the fifth day of their voyage, and were reaching chillier climes.

She walked briskly along the deck to stimulate her circulation, wishing her fellow passengers a good morning. The gentlemen tipped their hats and the ladies returned her greeting, commenting on the change in the weather.

At the end of the deck she saw a seaman leaning over the railing with a rope in his hands. Curious as to what he could be doing, she went over to the side of the deck to watch him. As she drew closer she saw that he was lowering a pail over the side of the ship, letting out the coil of rope as the pail descended towards the water.

'What are you doing?' she asked him curiously.

He turned towards her briefly. 'Taking the water temperature, miss,' he said, before turning back to his task.

'Will the pail reach?' she asked, looking down at the sea and trying to gauge the length of the rope attached to it. It seemed a long way to the water.

'Not with this breeze it won't,' he said gruffly, as the pail banged against the side of the ship. 'Not even with the pail being weighted.'

'It's a long way down to the surface,' she said, as she leaned over the rail to get a better look.

'That it is. It's seventy-five feet, miss.'

It looked all of that. The waves were dwarfed by the ship,

and, being so far below, looked like little more than ripples on a mill pond.

The seaman began to reel in the pail, coiling the rope in his hand as he did so. Then, taking hold of the pail, he went over to a stand pipe and filled it with water before putting a thermometer into it and taking the temperature.

'Is it very cold?' asked Emilia.

'Colder than usual,' he said. 'I shouldn't wonder if we don't come across ice later today.'

Ice was a feature of ocean voyages, or so, at least, Pansy had said, and Emilia found herself wondering if she would see any ice floes. She rather hoped she would. She was enjoying her journey, and she reflected that she would have a lot to tell her godmother when she finally arrived in Ireland.

She resumed her walk along the deck. It was busy, as usual, with people playing quoits or taking the air. There were fewer people sitting today, she noticed. Even out of the wind it was cold. However, she enjoyed being outside. It might be cold, but the wind brought a glow to her cheeks, and she found the sea air invigorating.

After a while she began to notice the other passengers leaving the deck and glanced at her watch. It was almost time for divine service. She followed them inside. There were a number of people heading towards the first-class dining room, where the divine service was to be held. She chose a seat close to the piano, then slipped off her coat and hung it over the back of her chair before looking about her.

To her relief, Carl was not there. It was becoming increasingly difficult for her to meet him with equanimity, and she was glad she did not have anything further to try her self-control.

After a few minutes Captain Smith entered the room. Emilia had often seen the captain walking about the ship, and had wished him a good morning or a good afternoon on several occasions, but this was her first opportunity to spend any great length of time in his presence. As he walked down the room, she thought how well he looked. His white hair, white moustache and full beard gave him an air of solidity. His uniform was smart and commanded respect. With its peaked cap, well-cut coat, brass buttons and polished shoes it fit in with everything else on *Titanic*, looking fresh and attractive. On his sleeve were four gold stripes denoting his rank.

He greeted the passengers affably, before he took his place at the front of the congregation.

Just before the service began, Pansy slipped into the room and sat down next to Emilia with Robert beside her. 'Good morning, did you sleep well?' she asked.

'Yes, very well,' said Emilia.

'So did I. I slept like a top. It's the sea air. It always puts me out like a light.'

Emilia exchanged greetings with Robert, who had settled himself down next to Pansy, and who then took up his hymn book and idly turned the pages, as he waited for the service to begin.

'We're so lucky to have Captain Smith,' said Pansy, as she turned her eyes forward. 'He's the best captain there is. Robert and I have sailed under him before. Some people won't sail under anyone else. They call him the millionaires' captain, you know, because he always captains the best ships. But then it's not surprising. He's steady, and he's safe. I asked him once about his years at sea, and do you know what he said? He said they'd been uneventful. Isn't that the best thing for a captain to say? He's never been in any accident worth speaking of, he told me. In fact, I've heard him saying so many times.'

'Yes, we're in safe hands, all right,' said Robert. 'Smith's an experienced man. He's been making the Atlantic crossing for years.'

The conversation gradually dwindled into silence and the service began. It was a simple ceremony, but it was conducted with dignity. Captain Smith had a wonderful presence and a fine voice. As the service progressed, Emilia could see why people liked to travel with him. There was an air of calm assurance about him which promoted a feeling of confidence in those who saw or heard him.

At last the service was over.

The congregation thanked the captain, then began to drift out of the dining room and go their separate ways.

'I'm surprised there is no lifeboat drill,' said Pansy as they left the dining room. 'There's always a drill on the first Sunday of a voyage. I can't think why Captain Smith didn't hold one today.'

'He doesn't need to,' laughed Robert. 'This ship's unsinkable. What does he want to hold a lifeboat drill for, on an unsinkable ship?'

'Is it really unsinkable?' asked Pansy.

'Of course it is,' replied Robert. 'I heard one of the deck hands saying so earlier. One of the passengers asked him, "Is this ship really unsinkable?" and he said, "Yes, lady, God himself could not sink this ship".'

Pansy laughed. 'Oh, Robert!'

'It's true. Besides, there's no way a ship could sink these days,' Robert went on. 'Even Captain Smith thinks so. Don't you remember what he said, on the maiden voyage of *Adriatic*?'

'Now you mention it, yes, I do,' said Pansy. 'We sailed on *Adriatic*'s maiden voyage as well,' explained Pansy to Emilia. 'It was a splendid voyage. I was wearing my dark red coat and ribboned hat, I remember, as we arrived in New York. Captain Smith said he couldn't imagine any condition which would cause a ship to founder. I remember his exact words. He said modern shipbuilding had gone beyond that.'

'I'm glad to hear it,' said Emilia with a smile.

They chatted for a few more minutes, and then Emilia excused herself, arranging to meet Pansy and Robert again for dinner that evening. She returned to her stateroom, intending to deposit her coat before heading for the library.

Hardly had she hung away her coat and tidied her hair, however, repairing the damage caused by her walk along the deck, when there was a knock at the door. To her surprise, when she opened it, she found Mrs Latimer standing there.

'Mrs Latimer. What a pleasant surprise. Do, please, come in,' said Emilia, welcoming Mrs Latimer into the room.

'Thank you, dear. I don't mind if I do.'

Her step was light, her cheeks were rosy, and she seemed full of life.

'It's a good thing you're here,' said Mrs Latimer, as Emilia offered her a seat. 'I called a few times yesterday but you were out.'

'I was exploring the ship,' Emilia said. 'Would you like some tea, or coffee?' she asked, once Mrs Latimer had sat down.

'Oh, yes, I'd like a cup of coffee,' she said. 'It seems a long time since I had my breakfast.'

Emilia rang for Mrs McLaren, her stewardess, then sat down opposite Mrs Latimer.

'This is nice,' said Mrs Latimer, looking appreciatively round the sitting room.

'Isn't it?' agreed Emilia, following her gaze and taking in the elaborately moulded fireplace and the elegant chairs. 'I knew *Titanic* was magnificent but I never imagined my sitting room would be so sumptuous.'

'And these chairs are comfy,' said Mrs Latimer, settling herself back in her seat. 'Now, it seems to me these ships are getting better all the time.'

'I keep having to remind myself I'm on a ship at all,' said Emilia with a smile.

'I know just what you mean. It's got so many libraries and cafés, it's like being in a town instead of on a ship. But it's a good thing I've found you in at last. I've been wanting to talk to you,' said Mrs Latimer.

She broke off as the stewardess entered with a tray of coffee. The coffee was in a silver coffee pot, and next to it were cups and saucers, a cream jug and sugar bowl, all in fine Crown Derby china.

'Will there be anything else, miss?' asked Mrs McLaren.

'No, thank you,' said Emilia. 'That will be all.'

Once Mrs McLaren had gone, Emilia poured out two cups of coffee.

When both ladies had taken a sip, Mrs Latimer said, 'Do you know, it's a good thing you came into my cabin on Thursday and said that Dr Allerton was a fraud. I didn't have

101

a chance to thank you properly over dinner, what with Mr Ismay and Mr Andrews being there, but it's made a big difference to my life. Carl's got rid of the doctor, and I can do as I like. I can't remember when I had such a good time.'

They fell easily into conversation about *Titanic* and all the wonderful things there were to do on board. The conversation then progressed to Mrs Latimer's life in New York, and the difficulty she had had in fitting in to her new circumstances in life before she had settled and started to enjoy herself as much as her low spirits had allowed.

'I'm very proud of Carl,' she said, 'but it was hard making friends in a new place, especially when I'd never been anywhere so grand in all my life. I liked my terrace house, but Carl wanted me to have something better. Not that I'm complaining, but I didn't think it was better myself. There was always something going on and everyone was always so neighbourly when we lived in Southampton. We helped each other. We had to. Things were hard. Then away we went to America and it was all very different. I never had to go shopping or make the meals. It was easy, but it was lonely.'

Emilia could well imagine it. When she had been growing up she had lived in a lovely big house, but it had been in a small village where everyone knew everyone, and where the same families had lived for generations. Then, when she had moved to Southampton, she and Aunt Clem had lived in a terrace house where neighbourliness had been the rule. But to go to live in a big house in a large community, not knowing anyone, must have been difficult.

'Well, of course I tried to get to know the neighbours,' said Mrs Latimer, 'but they pretended they weren't in and didn't come to see me. Well, all except one of them. She used to come and see me.'

'That was nice of her,' said Emilia encouragingly.

'Well, no, it wasn't.' Mrs Latimer pulled a face. 'In all my life I'd never met anyone like her, and a good thing, too. She wanted to make me squirm. She asked me how I was feeling, and pretended to be friendly, but really she came to tell me I wasn't one of her sort. "You were a lot more comfortable in your last house, I'm sure," she said to me. Well, it was true, but I wasn't going to tell her so. "It's so difficult to move out of one's own sphere in life," she said. "I expect you don't know what to do with yourself. It must be so difficult if you don't play the piano, or paint, or sketch. You must wish you were still scrubbing floors".'

'The cheek!' exclaimed Emilia.

Mrs Latimer nodded. 'Well, of course you're right, dear, but I was feeling so low I let her get away with it.'

'She sounds dreadful,' said Emilia.

'That's about the size of it,' Mrs Latimer agreed. 'She used to tell me about her Evelyn – how beautiful she is, how clever, how all the men are wild for her – then ask about my own girls and saying, "How quaint," when I tell her how they're doing, or something even worse. I told her how happy Vicky was, always singing around the house, and do you know what she said? "I had a maid who used to do that. Of course, I trained her out of it in the end".'

'What a monster!' said Emilia.

Mrs Latimer chuckled, then shook her head. 'I shouldn't have let her get under my skin.'

Emilia looked at her enquiringly.

'Well, I've done something I shouldn't have,' said Mrs Latimer, looking sheepish.

'I don't believe you could ever do anything you shouldn't,' said Emilia reassuringly.

'You're a good girl, but I have, all the same. As soon as she heard Carl was taking me to Europe she paid me a visit and started giving me orders. "Evelyn loves Maison Worth," she said to me. "Charlie Worth is a couturier," she said, like she was talking to a child. "Yes, I know who Charlie Worth is," I said. "As a matter of fact, I bought one of his frocks for Vicky the last time I was over there." "Frocks?" she said, like she didn't know what I was talking about. "Oh, you mean gowns." Now would you believe, she ended by telling me I could bring some Worth gowns back for Evelyn.'

'Well!' exclaimed Emilia.

Mrs Latimer nodded her head. 'That's just how I felt. But

I was feeling low and so I didn't say anything. Well, away we went to Europe. Carl thought it would do me good. And it might have done, if I'd gone out and enjoyed myself, but I stayed in hotel rooms most of the time.' She shook her head. 'It's hard to believe I was so low. Anyway, when we got to Paris, Carl made them bring some frocks to the hotel so I could look them over. He wanted to buy some for his sisters. He's always been so good to them. He's always been good to us all. Well, I chose some frocks for my girls, all right. And then I did a mean thing.'

'I suppose you didn't buy Evelyn a gown,' said Emilia. 'But then, why should you? It's not as if you'd offered to buy her one.'

Mrs Latimer pursed her lips. 'You'll think me a very wicked old woman,' she said, 'but I did something worse. I did buy her one, a lovely frock, the prettiest in the whole collection.'

'I hardly see why that's mean,' said Emilia confused.

There was a twinkle in Mrs Latimer's eye. 'Well, now,' she said, trying to suppress her laughter, 'I bought the wrong size so it wouldn't fit her. Evelyn's a beefy girl, and it's far too small! Well, now, I shouldn't be laughing,' said Mrs Latimer, tears running down her cheeks. 'It wasn't a nice thing to do. It's wicked to give it to her, knowing she won't be able to get it on.' She sobered. 'I don't like the waste, though. I've been poor long enough to know it's a sin to be wasteful.'

'Can't you give the gown to one of your daughters?' asked Emilia.

Mrs Latimer shook her head. 'It's too small for them as well,' she said. 'They're fine girls, but well made. They're not beefy like Evelyn, but they're not little sylphs like you.'

Her expression suddenly changed, becoming thoughtful. 'Well, do you know, it would be just the thing for you,' she said, as though she'd just thought of it. She brightened. 'That's it. I'll give it to you.'

'I couldn't possibly accept it,' began Emilia, taken aback.

'Why not? If you have it, it won't be wasteful, and I won't feel mean for buying it. It's such a pretty frock. It's got beads all over the bodice, and don't they shine! You'll look lovely in it. Say you'll have it, dear.'

'Well . . .'

Emilia was torn. On the one hand she wanted to help Mrs Latimer, and the gown sounded like a dream come true, but on the other hand she did not feel she could possible accept such a generous gift.

'It would show those old biddies a thing or two,' said Mrs Latimer. 'In all my life I've never heard anything worse than what they were saying the other night. "What's she wearing? Her grandmother's dress?",' she said, mimicking some of the comments that had followed Emilia when she had worn Aunt Clem's old gown.

'That wasn't the worst,' confided Emilia. 'The night before, I wore a home-made dress. They amused themselves by wondering if I'd know which cutlery to use, and whether I'd drink out of the finger bowl.'

At the thought of it, she was sorely tempted to accept the dress.

'Then that's that,' said Mrs Latimer.

Emilia made her decision. 'It's very kind of you . . .'

'Good. A bit of kindness to set against a bit of unkindness. What could be better than that?'

'Thank you,' said Emilia. 'I accept.'

'I'll send Miss Epson round with it.'

The clock on the mantelpiece chimed the hour.

'Is that the time?' said Mrs Latimer. 'I didn't know how late it was getting, I've been enjoying myself so much. Now I have to go. I said I'd meet Carl in the café for lunch.'

She said goodbye, then left Emilia with happy thoughts.

A Worth gown! She could hardly believe it. She had always been an admirer of the great couturier. She and Aunt Clem had often poured over his clothes in *La Mode Illustrée*, and the idea that she would soon be wearing one of his creations was exhilarating. She did not have long to wait to see it. Ten minutes later, Miss Epson arrived with a large box.

'Oh, I'm so glad you're going to wear the dress,' she sighed. 'It's so beautiful, and it will look lovely with your golden hair. Oh, dear, I shouldn't be standing here gossiping. I must be getting back to Mrs Latimer in case she wants me.'

She left Emilia alone with the box. Unable to resist, Emilia opened it. Swathes of tissue paper met her eyes. Carefully she opened them to reveal the most beautiful gown she had ever seen. The beading on the bodice was intricate, and sparkled in the light. The waist was high, following the fashionable Empire line. The skirt was indeed beautiful, falling in a column to the floor. But it was the colour that Emilia loved most. She picked up the gown and carried it over to the mirror, holding it up in front of herself. It was a rich blue that brought out the full beauty of her creamy complexion and her sapphire eyes.

There would be no jeering remarks directed towards her clothes tonight. Even in such exalted company, she would be wearing the most beautiful gown in the dining room. She could hardly wait!

After lunch, a telegraph arrived from Charlie:

Dear Emilia,

What wonderful news. I'm delighted to hear you're on board *Titanic*. Julia and I will meet you on the pier. She's a marvellous girl, Emilia. I love her very much, and so will you. We're both looking forward to seeing you and we insist on you staying with us whilst you're in New York. Julia wants to take you round all the best shops and I want to find out what's been happening in England since I left.

Love from
Charlie

The telegraph brought back warm memories of Charlie. He sounded more mature than the last time she had seen him. Falling in love with Julia, not to mention taking a job in antiques, seemed to have done him good. The engagement was clearly a happy one, and as he was making a success of his new job, she thought the move to America had been an excellent idea. However, her pleasure in his telegraph and in his invitation to stay was mixed with doubts. Would she be safe with him? Or would Barker or Silas Montmorency try to abduct her in New York?

She thought again of Carl's offer. It was very tempting. But she knew that if she stayed with him she would not be able to keep her feelings in check. No, it was far better to stay with Charlie. Besides, she was looking forward to seeing him. She had not seen him for years, not since her parents' death, and she, like him, wanted to catch up on all the news. And of course she wanted to get to know Julia. Once in New York she was sure she would have an enjoyable time. She would renew her friendship with Charlie, meet Julia, make an account of all the new sights and sounds, and then regale her godmother with them when she finally reached Ireland.

And once she was away from Carl Latimer, she told herself bracingly, she would put him out of her mind for good.

Eight

Emilia's eyes sparkled as she looked in the mirror. Mrs McLaren had kindly helped her to dress, and now here she was in the most exquisite gown she'd ever seen, with her mother's pearls around her throat, looking every bit as though she belonged in a first-class stateroom on board *Titanic*.

She pulled on her evening gloves, then patting her hair one last time, she left her stateroom and made her way through the ship until she came to the Grand Staircase. It was lit up in spectacular style. The electric lights shone and dazzled, bringing the carved wood of the banisters alive with a warm glow. Below her was a crowd of elegantly-dressed people, the women dressed in just the sort of gowns she and Aunt Clem had enjoyed poring over in *La Mode Illustrée*. She saw minutely-pleated gowns obviously designed by Fortuny, together with draped gowns by Poiret and others that bore all the hallmarks of Maison Worth. The colours were rich and glowing, and brilliant shades of emerald, cerise and royal blue competed with bright flames and golds. The gentlemen's clothes provided a foil, their white shirts, white bow ties and white waistcoats being teamed with black trousers and tail-coats.

At the foot of the stairs was Mrs Latimer. Next to her was Carl. He was resplendent in evening dress. His broad shoulders and long legs suited the clothes, showing their fine cut. With Carl and Mrs Latimer was a middle-aged couple. As she began to descend the staircase, Carl looked up and saw her.

She felt a flutter in her breast and her heart started to beat more quickly. He was staring, and as his eyes ran over her, she was aware of the fact that his glance was admiring. She hesitated on the landing, feeling ridiculously pleased, and yet at the same time suddenly self-conscious.

He walked towards her, climbing the stairs, his eyes fixed on her as though he saw no one else. 'You look beautiful,' he said.

His voice was low and husky, and she felt a shiver run down her spine.

'Thank you,' she said.

'Will you join us for dinner?' he asked. 'My mother and I are entertaining a small party at our table and we would love you to join us.'

She felt a deep regret. She would have liked nothing better than to dine with him, perilous though it might be, but she had promised Pansy and Robert she would join them.

'I'm afraid that won't be possible. I'm engaged to dine with the Wainfleets,' she said.

'If that's the only problem, I'll invite them to join us, too.'

He gave her his arm, and she rested her hand lightly on it. Even that small contact sent shivers through her body. Then together they walked down the stairs.

'Well, you do look lovely,' said Mrs Latimer, kissing her on the cheek. 'I knew that frock would fit you, but I never knew it would suit you like that. You look lovely, dear.'

Emilia disclaimed the compliment, but could not help being pleased: she felt beautiful tonight.

'Miss Cavendish was due to dine with the Wainfleets,' said Carl to his guests. 'I have suggested the three of them join us for dinner.'

'Well, what a good idea,' said Mrs Latimer.

'Excellent,' said the lady.

'Miss Cavendish, may I present Mr and Mrs Thirske?' said Carl, performing the introductions.

Just as he finished the introductions, Pansy and Robert descended the staircase, and he invited them cordially to join his party.

Pansy's eyebrows rose with excitement. 'Oh, yes, that sounds very nice. We'd be honoured, wouldn't we, Robert?'

Robert professed himself very happy, and they all went into the dining room together.

'Emilia, you look ravishing,' said Pansy, as the two ladies took their place at table. 'Where did you get that gown?'

Emilia told her the story as they settled themselves, whilst the Thirskes occupied Carl and his mother with a conversation about the play they had seen in Southampton before boarding the boat.

'Do you know, I think your beau's one of the most handsome men on the ship – after Robert, of course,' Pansy said in a low voice to Emilia.

'He's not my beau,' protested Emilia.

'No? Why else would he ask us to dine with him?' asked Pansy.

'Because I helped his mother. He's grateful,' Emilia told her, explaining the circumstances.

'He doesn't look like a man who's grateful to me,' said Pansy. 'He looks like a man who's in love.'

'You couldn't be more wrong,' said Emilia, flushing. 'Mr Latimer has no feelings for me beyond gratitude, and perhaps a little friendship.'

There was something in her voice that put an end to Pansy's banter, and she was relieved to find that Pansy allowed her to turn the conversation into more general channels.

As Emilia glanced at the splendid menu she thought how much had changed since the last time she had sat at Carl's table. Then she had had feelings for him, it was true, but now they were so much deeper. And no matter how much she told herself she should not be encouraging them, she found she could not drive them away. He was everything she had ever wanted in a man, without even knowing it. He was strong yet tender; powerful but not brutal. He was intriguing and mesmerizing and wonderfully desirable, she thought, as she glanced at him across the table.

And he was also spoken for. With a sinking feeling she remembered the magazine article, and the words of Mrs Gisborne. Carl was shortly to become engaged to Miss Isabelle Stott.

Emilia was about to turn her eyes towards her menu again when he looked up, as if feeling her eyes on him. She tried to look away, but she could not do it. Their eyes held. There was something magnetic in his glance which caught her fast.

Even when Mr Thirske spoke to him he did not look away. 'We didn't see you at divine service this morning, Latimer.'

He answered Mr Thirske, but his eyes never left Emilia's as he said, 'No. I'm afraid I overslept.'

'Late night?' queried Mr Thirske.

Carl drew his eyes away from Emilia. She could feel what a struggle it had been for him.

'Something like that,' he said, unwillingly giving Mr Thirske his full attention.

'I hope the card sharps didn't get you,' said Mr Thirske ruefully. 'I ran across one of them our first night out from Southampton. Of course, I didn't know who he was at the time. I thought he was just a fellow passenger. He seemed so respectable. But that's his stock in trade, I suppose. He let me win at first, but just as I was getting comfortable he stung me for a large sum.'

Carl nodded sympathetically. 'There are always a group of them on board any notable sailing.'

'Still, I've learnt my lesson. No more gambling for me,' said Mr Thirske. 'Early to bed and early to rise, that's the ticket.'

'I thought the service was lovely,' said Mrs Thirske. 'Captain Smith has such a wonderful voice. So resonant.'

The ladies agreed.

'It must be a marvellous life being a captain,' went on Mrs Thirske. 'Walking around and looking smart and going to dinner with the richest, most famous people in America. He's dining in the à la carte restaurant this evening, courtesy of the Wideners, or so I hear – George Widener's the head of a banking and railroad family, you know,' she said.

'It's true, there are perks, but he has a lot of responsibility as well,' her husband reminded her.

'Oh, yes, but not on *Titanic*. What can go wrong on an

unsinkable ship? He'll be sorry to leave all this behind when he retires, I'm sure.'

'I don't know,' said Pansy. 'We're sailing into dangerous waters. They call this part of the ocean Devil's Hole.'

'What nonsense,' said Robert affably.

'It isn't nonsense, it's true,' she returned, unperturbed. 'My stewardess was telling me about it, and she should know. She's crossed the Atlantic many times before. A lot of her ladies are nervous when they reach this stretch of water, she told me. It's a dreadful place for accidents. Icebergs can drift down this far, and they can hole a ship.'

'An ordinary ship, maybe,' said Mr Thirske, 'but not *Titanic.*'

'It's certainly cold enough for icebergs,' said Robert, taking up the theme. 'We took a turn on deck before coming into the dining room and the temperature's dropped noticeably. It's going to be a cold night.'

Whilst the others talked, Emilia studiously buried her head in her menu. She was afraid to look up in case she met Carl's eye. But once she had ordered she could no longer hide, and before her silence could become noticeable to the rest of the dinner party she joined in the conversation.

'I've never seen an iceberg.'

'They're beautiful if you see them in the right light,' said Carl. It seemed as though he was speaking only to her. 'They can appear to be blue, gold, or even red, instead of the white you might expect.'

'Do you think we'll see any tonight?' asked Mrs Latimer.

'We might see a few, but only in the distance,' said Carl, now glancing round the table and including everyone in his remarks. 'The ship will steer clear of them. We're more likely to see ice floes, I should think. They're common at this time of year.'

The first course was served. Conversation dwindled, reviving again between courses, as they discussed everything from the speed of their crossing to the latest novels. The food was excellent, and in the background the music provided the perfect atmosphere as the orchestra played a lively selection of tunes.

'Well, we'd better go and sit in the lounge so the men can have their cigars and brandies,' said Mrs Latimer, once dinner was over.

The ladies rose.

'That was a wonderful meal,' sighed Pansy, as they went into the lounge. Like the other rooms on the ship it was magnificent. Light and spacious, it had high ceilings and elaborate mouldings, and was decorated in Georgian style. The ladies engaged in desultory conversation about the latest fashions, but before long Mrs Latimer was stifling yawns and declaring herself ready for bed.

Pansy, too, declared her intention of retiring. She had some letters to write, she said. They departed, together with Miss Epson, and were soon followed by Mrs Thirske.

Emilia, however, was not tired. It was not yet half past eleven, and intrigued by the thought of seeing an iceberg she went out on to deck. There was no wind, but the air was cold. However, she only intended to stay outside for a few minutes, and wrapped her arms around herself to keep warm.

The ship looked magical. Light streamed from every porthole and every deck. Lanterns were hung along its entire length. It was like a fairy ship, strung with glow worms illuminating the dark night sky.

She looked out across the water. It was as calm as a mill pond, and its dark depths reflected the lights. The ship was still going at a good pace, and she was reassured by this, for if the captain had felt there was any danger he would have slowed down. She could not see any ice. She had hoped to see an iceberg glowing with a blue or silver light in the starlight, but there was nothing. She shivered, and decided she must go in.

She was just about to do so when she became aware that there was someone behind her. She felt her skin prickle, and without even having to look round she knew who it was. There was only one man who could light up the air with such a powerful electrical charge.

Carl.

'It's a beautiful night,' he said.

Amanda P. Grange

She took a deep breath and turned round to face him. His face was shadowed, but one side of it was illuminated by the ship's lights, and she was aware of his high cheekbones and smooth skin. She had an urge to reach out and trail her fingers down his strong face, letting them linger on his jaw before brushing his lips. But she could not give in to such an impulse. To help her fight it she folded her arms.

'It is,' she agreed. Deliberately turning her eyes skywards, her gaze traced the heavens. 'It's so peaceful out here, away from the hustle and bustle of normal life.'

He nodded. 'It's as though the rest of the world doesn't exist.'

It was true. Sheltered by the darkness, cut off from the noise that existed inside the ship, they seemed like the only two people left in the world. It was a wonderful feeling.

It was also unnerving.

Carl exerted a strange power over her. If she was to forget where she was she would be in danger of succumbing to it. Her only hope lay in reminding herself that she was on a ship full of people and that at any moment one of them might come out on to the deck.

The wind blew, and she shivered. But before she could say she must go in, he had stripped off his jacket and he was by her side, wrapping it round her bare shoulders.

'Here.'

She accepted it gratefully. It was warm with his body heat, and it contained the unmistakeable scent of him, a mixture of expensive cologne and masculinity. She nestled into it, then lifted her face to thank him ... and the words died on her lips. His hands were still on her shoulders, and as she looked into his eyes, she was lost. They were so deep they drew her in. She saw his feelings as clearly as though they'd been written on his face in letters a mile high. He was going to kiss her.

She knew what she had to do. She had to pull away, step out of his grasp, thank him politely for his jacket, tell him it was not necessary, return it to him and go back inside. But she could not do it. The night was so magical and his presence was so overwhelming that she simply stood there, in the

114

grip of a nameless spell, and raised her face to his.

He took her chin between his finger and thumb, and then bent his head, and brushed her lips with his own. She could feel the slight roughness of the stubble around his mouth, and she found it stimulating. She responded, and he took her into his arms and kissed her.

It was a deep, slow sensuous kiss, such as she had never experienced before. Her knees buckled, and if his arms had not been around her waist she would have fallen. He pulled her closer and her arms instinctively rose and slid around his neck. She ran her fingers through his hair, revelling in its sleekness, and returning his kiss with a passionate intensity she had never dreamed she possessed.

He pulled away briefly, whispering endearments as he nuzzled her ear, then reclaimed her mouth with his own. He deepened the kiss, and as her lips parted she felt the sweet invasion of his tongue. She had never dreamt an embrace could be so all-consuming. His masculine scent made her senses reel, the feel of his hair set her heart pounding, and the taste of his lips made her hungry for more. He was swamping all her senses. Sight, scent, sound, taste and touch were full of him. He was her whole world.

Overwhelmed by the sensations coursing through her she lost all track of time, knowing nothing but the pressure of his body and the sweet insistence of his lips.

How long it would have gone on for she did not know, but the sound of voices called her back to reality. Other passengers, lured by the stars and the stillness, were coming out on to the deck, and although they were further down, they had reminded her of the real world and all its complications.

She must have been mad to let him kiss her, she thought, as she pulled away from him, her feelings a mass of confusion. She had meant to avoid him and instead she had surrendered herself, giving herself to him willingly and welcoming his kiss. For she could not hide from herself that she had welcomed it. It had seemed so right that she had wanted it, and enjoyed it, and even worse, longed to feel it again. After her experience with Silas Montmorency – after the day he had grabbed her and covered his mouth with her own – she had wondered if she would ever enjoy a man's caresses. She had hated the feel of Silas's mouth on hers, and the feel of his arms around her had driven her mad with panic and the desire to escape. But when Carl had taken her in his arms she had not wanted to escape. And when he had kissed her, she had kissed him back, matching his passion with a passion of her own. She had forgotten herself, lulled by the sea and the stars and the faint strains of music coming from the dining room, but she must not forget herself again. Now, more than ever, she must be on her guard.

She was under no illusions about Carl's feelings. She was, to him, a light indulgence, something with which to pass the time whilst he sailed across the Atlantic, but to her he was something more. He touched her in ways she had never been touched before. He intrigued her, interested her, compelled her. And he attracted her like no other man. But it was madness to give in to it.

She pulled herself together.

'I must go.'

She turned away from him but he caught her hand as she did so.

'I've frightened you,' he said, pulling her towards him. 'I'm sorry. That was not my intention. Stay.'

His voice was low and husky, and she was in danger of weakening all over again.

She made a determined effort to control her reaction to him. 'No, you haven't frightened me,' she said. 'But this was a mistake. It must never happen again.'

He raised his eyebrows. 'May I ask why not?'

'You know perfectly well why not,' she said.

'No. I don't.'

'Mr Latimer, this is neither the time nor the place for such a discussion,' she said, glancing along the deck to where several gentlemen were standing by the railings, smoking their cigars.

'Then the sooner you tell me what is the matter, the better,' he said. 'Did I offend you in some way?'

'No.' She hesitated. 'Yes.'

'You're not making this easy for me.' There was a hint of exasperation in his voice. 'I have no wish to distress you. Only tell me why you say it can never happen again, and I will make sure it doesn't.'

With his hand clasping hers, and his eyes locked on to her own, it was difficult for her to concentrate. It would have been so easy to give herself up to the sensations that were coursing through her, but she knew she must not do it.

She straightened her spine. 'Because you are about to become engaged,' she said.

'Engaged?' He was so surprised he stood back, dropping his hand to his side. 'Whatever gives you that idea?'

'Mrs Gisborne told me,' she said.

He let out a sigh. 'Did she indeed?'

'Yes. She did. And I saw the news of your impending engagement in a magazine.'

He ran his fingers through his hair. 'Emilia, I'm a wealthy man. I am hunted by mothers who want wealthy husbands for their daughters. I have been for the last three years. Mrs Gisborne's sister is one of those who hunts me. She has a daughter, Isabelle, a beautiful girl. It's true, I had considered marrying her, together with a number of other young women, all beautiful, elegant and well-connected. I was of an age to marry, and having forgotten what was important in life, I saw a marriage with one of them as the final rung on the ladder of my climb from poverty. But then I met you . . .'

She stepped back. 'Nevertheless, you are engaged, or as good as engaged, to her,' she said.

'I'm no such thing. Although I had seen Isabelle as a possible wife, I took great care to make sure I never misled her, or any of the other young women, by paying them undue atten-tion. The idea that I am about to offer her marriage is in her mother's imagination.'

'But the magazine?' asked Emilia.

'Mrs Stott wanted to manipulate me into proposing to Isabelle. She has a relative who works for a society maga-zine, and persuaded her to include a photograph of Isabelle and myself, with a caption saying we were shortly to become engaged. But it isn't so.'

She looked up into his eyes and saw that what he said was true.

'You reminded me of what was important in life. With you, I remembered what it was like to talk to someone who interested me, to spend time with someone who made life seem vibrant and meaningful.'

He stroked her cheek.

'With you I discovered what it was like to talk to a woman honestly, instead of having her flatter me and agree with everything I said.' His voice became husky. 'And with you I found out what it was like to have a woman tremble in my arms, not at the thought of my money, but at the touch of me, as a man.'

And then she was in his arms again, being crushed to his chest, and returning his kiss with a fire she had never dreamed she possessed.

Suddenly, there came the sound of a bell ringing.

She barely heard it.

It came again.

This time it began to penetrate her consciousness, and she opened her eyes.

It came a third time.

Carl released her, and they both looked in the direction of the sound. It was coming from the crow's nest.

'What is it?' she asked.

'It's a warning,' he said. 'It means there's something up ahead.'

Taking her hand, he led her over to the rail and they looked out to sea and saw an iceberg directly in front of them. It towered over the deck, dwarfing the ship with its size.

Emilia gasped. She had wanted to see an iceberg, but not at such close quarters, and definitely not in the path of the ship.

She squeezed Carl's hand.

'Don't worry,' he said. 'The ship will turn to avoid it.'

She heard a barking of orders coming from the bridge a

little further down the deck, and slowly the bow of the gigantic vessel began to veer to port. She held her breath. The iceberg was coming ever closer, and yet the ship was turning so slowly. Its enormous length worked against it. For one heart-stopping moment she feared it was not going to escape a collision. Unconsciously, she drew closer to Carl. He put his arm reassuringly around her shoulders.

And then the bow turned still more, and she let out a pent-up breath as she realized the ship was going to miss the iceberg. The bow turned, and *Titanic* slipped majestically past.

She relaxed. It had been an anxious moment, but now it was over.

Or so she had thought. Suddenly, at that moment there came a scraping sound, and a curious shuddering sensation, as though the ship was rolling over a thousand marbles. Then there was a sudden silence as the engines stopped.

It was eerie. *Titanic* was suddenly like a ghost ship, adrift on the sea. In the darkness of the night, the silence was deafening.

'Why have we stopped?' she asked Carl. 'I thought we missed the iceberg?'

Carl shrugged. 'We've probably just thrown a propeller,' he said.

Emilia was comforted.

There came a coughing, spluttering sound, as though the engines were trying to start again, and then silence once more prevailed.

'How long will it take—' began Emilia.

She was cut off by a mighty roar, like the sound of a hundred trains rushing through a tunnel, and the rest of her words were drowned out in the deafening noise. Instinctively she put her hands over her ears.

'It's just the steam from the exhausts,' Carl shouted, to make himself heard over the din. 'If they've had to stop the engines when the ship was going at twenty knots, they will have to let the steam escape.'

'It sounds terrible,' she said, shouting too. 'I wonder if

we'll be able to see what's happened if we go over to the starboard side?'

It was on the starboard side of the ship that the iceberg had passed by.

'We might as well have a look.'

Taking her by the hand he led her across the deck. They passed close by the bridge, where there was a flurry of activity. Captain Smith was just arriving from the chart room to take command.

'Close the emergency doors,' she heard him say.

'They're already closed, sir,' said Mr Murdoch.

'Send to the carpenter and tell him to sound the ship,' said the captain.

Emilia remembered Mrs Thirske's words about Captain Smith not having any responsibility, but the weight of his position was now brought home to her. On his shoulders lay the decisions that must be taken in the aftermath of the incident. Judging by his voice, though, it must have been trivial. He was collected and calm.

They carried on making their way round to the starboard side of the ship. They could see the huge cliff of ice they had so narrowly avoided. It looked beautiful. In the starlight it was phosphorescent, a ghostly mountain floating away from the ship and disappearing off the stern.

Then her attention was caught by something on the deck. Ice.

'We must have hit the iceberg after all,' she said, glancing at the huge chunks which lay gleaming on the deck. She leaned over the railing and looked down at the side of the ship. 'I don't see any damage.'

'The iceberg must have grazed the ship below the water line,' said Carl.

'That explains the shuddering,' agreed Emilia. 'Will it have made a hole, do you think?'

'It's impossible to say. *Titanic*'s well built. It might just have scratched the hull. But Captain Smith will need to assess the damage before we move on.'

'That must be why we have stopped.'

She bent down and picked up a piece of the ice. To her surprise, it was not just frozen water, but had bits of rock and soil embedded in it. It was intensely cold; so much so that she gasped and dropped it again.

A few people were now appearing from below, disturbed from their sleep by the juddering sensation that had spread throughout the ship. They wore coats thrown hastily over their nightclothes, and on their feet they wore slippers.

One of the men strolled over to Carl. 'Do you know what happened?' he asked. 'We felt a judder downstairs. It woke us up. Were you on deck at the time?'

'Yes. I thought at first we'd thrown a propeller, but now I'm not so sure. From the ice on the deck, it looks as though we must have hit the iceberg.'

'I think so, too. I went into the smoking room to see what the opinion was there, but the men were still playing cards and seemed to have no interest in what had taken place.'

'It was only a glancing blow. We must have stopped to see if there's any serious damage been done,' said another gentleman. 'It might delay us a bit, but we've been making good speed on the crossing and even if we have to stay here an hour or two whilst repairs get under way we should still arrive on time.'

'I'll say we've been making good speed,' said a third. 'It's the fastest crossing I've ever made. 490 miles, wasn't it, from noon on the 11th to noon on the 12th?'

'494,' his wife corrected him. 'Then 519 miles between noon on the 12th and noon on the 13th, and 546 miles between noon on the 13th and noon on the 14th.'

'Marvellous woman, my wife,' he said proudly, putting his arm round her. 'She's been talking to the captain. She takes it all in.'

His wife looked pleased.

Some of the other passengers who had come out on deck were now playing with the ice, using it as a football, or, like Emilia, picking it up, before discovering how cold it was and tossing it from hand to hand.

'I think I'll take it home as a souvenir!' joked a young man. 'The wife would like it.'

'Put it in your whiskey!' laughed his friend.

There was an air of high spirits as the seasoned travellers on the ship took the accident in their stride.

'This is a bit of excitement, what?' said a fourth gentleman, puffing on his cigar. Unlike some of the other passengers, he was not dressed in his night clothes, but was still dressed in evening clothes. He was evidently enjoying himself. 'I've crossed the Atlantic nigh on fifty times and nothing interesting has ever happened before. It will be something for the newspapers to write about when we get back home.'

'It won't make half a column,' returned another gentleman, laughing, as he kicked a piece of ice across the deck. 'There's nothing to it. By this time tomorrow everyone will have forgotten all about it. Still, the sooner they fix the problem the better, whatever it is. There's an infernal racket from the steam.' He looked at the sky. 'It's a good thing it's a lovely night. There's not a breath of wind. It'll make it easier to carry out repairs. I think I'll stay on deck and see what happens.'

'How long do you think we'll be stopped for?' asked his wife.

'Not long. Once the captain's found out how much damage there is he'll get it fixed and we'll be on our way again.'

'It's cold out here,' she said. 'I'm going back to my stateroom. There's nothing to see, and I need my sleep.'

Over the noise, Emilia heard another order from the bridge. Interested to find out exactly what had happened, she drew closer, meaning to ask one of the officers what was wrong, but they were very busy and she did not like to interrupt them.

'Put the pumps to work,' she heard the captain say.

She was startled. If the pumps were being put to work, then the ship must have taken on water.

She went over to Carl, who was still by the ship's rail. 'I think the damage must be worse than we realized. I've just heard the captain telling the crew to start using the pumps.'

'Then it seems as though the ship must have been holed,' said Carl with a frown.

'Thank goodness for the bulkheads,' she returned. 'At least we know the ship won't sink.'

'I don't know,' said a lady who had just that moment come on deck. She was dressed in her nightgown, with a coat on top. 'I've just seen Mr Andrews. He was taking the stairs three at a time, and when I asked him if everything was all right he brushed me off and didn't give me any reply. It's worried me.'

'Oh, that means nothing,' said the first gentleman. 'This ship's his baby. I've heard him say so. He can't bear the thought of a scratch on her, that's all. He'll be as polite as anything by morning again, and apologizing for rushing straight past.'

Crew members started appearing on deck.

Emilia was surprised . . . and then began to feel the first stirrings of disquiet. There was a purposeful air about them, which showed they were there for a reason. Then she heard the order given: 'Uncover the lifeboats.'

One of the crew members caught sight of her face. 'Don't worry, it's nothing serious,' he said cheerily. 'It's just a precaution.'

He proceeded to pull the cover from the lifeboat at the side of the deck, whilst other crewmen began to operate the winches.

Emilia turned to Carl. 'Would they be uncovering the lifeboats if there wasn't any danger?' she asked.

'Probably,' he said, putting his hand on her arm. 'Don't worry. I'm sure it's nothing. The captain will have a procedure to follow, that's all.'

The touch of his hand was comforting. So, too, was the sound of his voice.

'There was no lifeboat practice this morning. It seems as though there will be one this evening, instead,' she said, lightening the situation.

More people were starting to come on deck, but now instead of wearing pyjamas and overcoats many of them were fully dressed, and over their coats they were wearing life jackets.

'It's just a precaution, miss,' explained one of the stewards

123

as he hurried past. 'We're telling everyone to put on their life vests, just to be on the safe side. Put something warmer on, if you don't mind, miss, and then put your life jacket on top of it, and come back on deck.'

'He's right,' said Carl. 'It's cold out here. You should be dressed properly. I'll take you back to your stateroom and you can put your coat and boots on.'

He put his arm round her shoulders and began guiding her back along the deck.

'It's all right,' she said, turning to face him. 'I can go by myself. You need to put your coat on, too, and you must see to your mother. She won't know what's happening and she will need someone to explain it to her.'

She slipped out of his jacket and handed it back to him.

He nodded. 'I'm sure there's no danger. Even so, I'd be happier if she was up on deck. I'll rouse both her and Miss Epson and tell them to get dressed. Meet me back here as soon as you can.'

'Very well.'

She hurried towards the stairs. The night air bit into her. She was wearing only a sleeveless evening gown and she was very cold. She wrapped her arms around herself, rubbing them as she hurried along the deck and down the stairs, back into the main body of the ship. As she did so, she passed people hurrying the other way. Some were dressed in their night-clothes. Others were fully dressed.

She made her way along the narrow but well lighted passage that led to her stateroom. Stewards were knocking on doors, telling people to get up.

'Dress warmly,' they were saying. 'It's just a precaution, there's nothing to worry about, but make sure you wear your life jacket.'

Sleepy passengers rubbed their eyes and asked each other what time it was. Some were curious, others were annoyed to be disturbed. Some flatly refused to get out of bed.

She finally reached her stateroom and went in . . . only to stand still in shock. Ice had come in through the porthole and was melting on the carpet.

Collecting herself, she went over to the wardrobe and took out a day dress. Slipping out of the beautiful but impractical Worth evening gown she put on her hard-wearing day dress, then put on her coat and changed into a sturdy pair of boots. Mrs McLaren, the stewardess, hurried in just as she was about to pull on her gloves.

'You'll need your life jacket,' she said.

She showed Emilia where it was stored, then helped her to put it on. It was made out of cork floats covered in canvas, and was thick and bulky, but fortunately it was large enough to put on over her coat. Mrs McLaren fastened it for her, tying the strings at her sides, before going into the next stateroom to help the passengers there.

'Nothing to worry about, but dress warmly, put on your life vests and go up to the boat deck,' came the voices of the stewards and stewardesses drifting through Emilia's door.

Dressed as warmly as possible, Emilia made her way back to the boat deck.

There were more people there now, and an air of curiosity prevailed. They were watching the crewmen, who had removed the lifeboat covers and were coiling the ropes in their hands, or turning the handles that operated the machinery for lowering the boats over the side. The cheerful sound of music accompanied them. The musicians had come out on to the deck and were playing ragtime tunes to entertain the passengers and crew. A number of crewmen with nothing better to do were pairing off and waltzing round the deck in time to the music, laughing and joking. Other crew members were standing about smoking.

Emilia looked for Carl but did not see him. It did not surprise her. If his mother had been asleep – and judging by Mrs Latimer's yawns after dinner, that would almost certainly have been the case – then he would have had to rouse her, after which he would have had to wait until both she and Miss Epson had dressed. It would probably be some time before he appeared on deck. She did, however, see Pansy.

'Emilia!' called Pansy, hurrying over to her. 'Isn't it exciting? Imagine hitting an iceberg. What an adventure.

There's some talk of putting us out in the boats. Goodness knows why. It's just a precaution, they say, but a precaution against what? I want to know. It's not as though *Titanic* can sink.'

Her breath misted in the cold air as she spoke.

'Absolutely,' said Robert. He rubbed his hands together. 'A lot of fuss about nothing, if you ask me. Still, I suppose it gives the crew something to do.'

As they stood talking together, one of the gentlemen next to them asked an officer casually, 'Any danger?'

'None at all, sir,' he replied brightly. 'We're just checking the damage, but it's unlikely to be anything much. Even if it turns out to be worse than we fear, we've got rockets on board to summon assistance. There's nothing to worry about. We're just getting the boats ready as a precaution.'

He hurried away.

'Told you so,' said Robert. 'This is just an interruption to the voyage. It'll soon be over and we can all go back to bed.'

One of the officers was now holding a megaphone. Standing next to a lifeboat, which had been lowered from the davits and now hung over the side of the ship on a level with the deck, he called out, 'Women and children!' Fortunately, the noise of the escaping steam had stopped and it was easy to hear him. 'Can I have the women and children over here?'

'Nonsensical idea,' said the lady next to Emilia. 'I'm not getting into a lifeboat. As if I'd leave the safety of the ship for a little wooden boat in the middle of the ocean. I'd as soon get into a cockleshell.'

'You're quite right,' laughed her husband. 'You'd have to be mad to get into one of those things. You'd catch your death of cold out there on the ocean in a little boat like that. *Titanic* can't sink. It's much safer on board.'

Very few people wanted to go. Emilia could understand why. It was a drop of seventy-five feet to the water, and the undertaking looked perilous.

One of the crewmen was busy setting off the first distress rocket. It boomed as it shot into the air and exploded into a mass of white stars. It was breathtaking, and it illuminated the sky and sea for miles around.

'Goodness,' said Pansy. 'It's like the 5th November! How pretty.'

'Women and children,' called the officer again.

'Go on, my dear,' said a gentleman to his wife. 'It's just a precaution, but I'd feel safer if you were off the ship.'

'No, I'd rather stay here with you,' she returned.

'Oh, very well,' he sighed.

Pansy, however, needed no coaxing. 'I don't mind going,' she said.

'What?' Robert was surprised.

'It looks exciting,' said Pansy. 'It will be something to tell them all about at home. Besides, this is my chance to talk to Miss Gibson.'

Miss Dorothy Gibson, the film star, was stepping into one of the boats, accompanied by her mother. She was being helped by a gentleman who was holding her hand. She stretched one foot out over the side of the ship and placed it in the lifeboat. Her other foot followed, but she did not relinquish the gentleman's hand.

'We don't go unless you do,' she said to him.

There were two gentlemen in her party. Emilia had seen them playing bridge together earlier that evening. The gentlemen looked at the half empty lifeboat and then at each other.

'What do you say?' asked one.

'What's the difference?' shrugged the other.

The gentlemen climbed in.

Pansy had by now seated herself in the boat, helped by Robert. 'Come on, Emilia,' she said as she arranged her coat round her.

'No.' Emilia shook her head. 'I want to wait for Carl.'

Pansy gave her a knowing look.

'I arranged to meet him, and I must do so,' said Emilia.

'Is there anyone else who'd like to get into the boat?' asked one of the officers.

'Robert, you come,' said Pansy.

He shook his head. 'Women and children first.'

'Don't be ridiculous,' she said. 'You can see as well as I can that none of the women want to come, and the boat's half empty. Besides, there are other gentlemen already in the boat. I can't think why you're making such a fuss. Anyone would think the ship was going to sink. All we're going to do is row round for half an hour and then get back on board.'

'Oh, very well,' said Robert.

He climbed aboard.

'Lower away!' came the call.

With a creaking of new ropes, they began to lower the boat. Emilia counted only twenty-eight men, women and crew on board. She saw their faces getting smaller and smaller as the boat was lowered down the side of the ship until it finally hit the sea. She could just make out Pansy's hat, with the glow of Robert's cigar next to it, and wondered whether Pansy would have a chance to talk to Dorothy Gibson as she hoped. Knowing Pansy, she thought it only too likely!

She watched as the boat began to pull away from the ship. It glided away on a sea so calm it could have been made out of glass.

It was a beautiful night, with not a breath of wind, and a clear sky. The cheerful strains of the orchestra playing ragtime music filled the air. With the intermittent booms of the rockets, and the white stars exploding overhead, there was a festive atmosphere.

Emilia glanced at her watch. It was 12.45, just over an hour since the ship had hit the iceberg, and about half an hour since Carl had gone below to help his mother. He should soon be returning to the deck.

She went round to the port side of the ship to see if he had already, perhaps, returned. Just as she was passing one of the gangways, a fireman staggered up from below. His arm was bleeding from a long gash.

A woman close to him looked horrified. 'Is there any danger?' she asked him hesitantly.

'Danger?' he yelled. 'I should just say so! It's hell down below. This ship will sink like a stone in ten minutes.'

He was obviously in a great deal of distress, but before Emilia could do anything to help him, First Officer Murdoch took charge. He was a firm man, and strong minded. He placed crew at the top of the gangways so that no one else could come up from below as the fireman was helped.

Emilia understood why. It would not do to have the passengers alarmed by such talk. Whether there was any dreadful danger she did not know. The fireman would obviously believe so if he himself had been wounded, but that did not mean it was so. He could simply have come from a part of the ship that had been badly damaged, whilst the rest of the ship remained intact. There did not seem to be any great danger. There was a slight list to the ship, it was true, but nothing very much. *Titanic* did not seem likely to sink. And to sink in ten minutes? No. Even so, the incident was unsettling.

There was no sign of Carl on the port side of the ship, so she returned to the starboard side. She wished he would come.

Her eyes travelled round the deck. She saw a number of other passengers, all talking in desultory fashion and discussing the untoward turn of events. She recognized Colonel Astor. He was with a number of other gentlemen. Some were smoking cigars and some were drinking brandies. They all seemed calm and collected.

Her eyes travelled on.

She saw Mrs McLaren, her stewardess, standing by lifeboat number five. Next to her was a man in a dressing gown and slippers. With a shock Emilia realized it was Mr Ismay. The last time she had seen him he had been dressed in his evening clothes, looking cheerful and gay. Now his face was strained.

'Get into the boat,' he was saying to Mrs McLaren and another stewardess.

'But we're not passengers,' Emilia heard Mrs McLaren protest. 'We're only members of the crew.'

He spoke firmly. 'Nevertheless you are women and I want you to get into the boat.'

With doubtful looks at each other, the stewardesses at last did as he said.

Emilia felt the stirrings of unease. Mr Ismay's face was

grave, and the fact that he was forcing the stewardesses to leave the ship made her fear the situation was worse than she had supposed.

Fortunately her thoughts were interrupted at that moment by a cry ringing out over the jumbled noise of conversation and officers' instructions being relayed through megaphones.

'Emilia!'

The voice belonged to Carl.

She turned round to see him heading towards her, with his mother on one arm and Miss Epson on the other. Both ladies were dressed warmly in thick coats, with stout shoes, muffs and gloves, and both were wearing life jackets. Carl, too, was warmly dressed with an overcoat, boots and life jacket.

'Well, what a lot of fuss and no mistake,' said Mrs Latimer as they drew close. 'Carl's telling me I've got to get in a lifeboat, but I don't like the look of them. They're too small. I'd sooner stay on the ship. There's nothing wrong with it as far as I can see. A bit of a tilt, maybe, but nothing much.'

A crewman hurried past and she called out to him, 'Is it really serious?'

'No, ma'am, there's no danger,' he said reassuringly. 'There's been some damage to the ship, but it's only trivial, and just in case it proves worse than we fear we've summoned four other ships by wireless. The first one will be here inside an hour.'

'You see,' she said to Carl. 'There's no use leaving the ship. If it's serious after all, the other ships will take us off when they get here. They'll be a lot safer than those cigar boxes,' she said, eyeing the lifeboats dubiously. Then she turned to Emilia. 'He'll listen to you. Tell him he's making a fuss.'

Emilia glanced at Carl, then back at Mrs Latimer. She did not want to cause alarm, but she was concerned. Mr Ismay's face and his insistence that the stewardesses must get in the boats, to say nothing of the fact that he, the White Star chairman, was personally helping people into the lifeboats, had begun to make her anxious. For the first time she thought it possible there might be some danger.

'I think it's a good idea,' said Emilia. 'Pansy and Robert have gone. So has Dorothy Gibson. It will be something to talk about when you get home.'

'Well, I suppose so,' sighed Mrs Latimer. 'I'd better go. You'll only bully me until I do,' she said to Carl. 'Miss Epson, you'd better get in first,' she went on, turning to her companion.

Chivvied along by Mr Ismay, and assisted by Carl and one of the crewmen, Miss Epson approached the side of the deck. 'Oh, dear,' she said nervously.

'Easy now,' said one of the crewmen. 'Nothing to fear. Just put your foot over the side and into the lifeboat. I've got you,' he said reassuringly, as she put one tentative foot into the boat whilst the other was still on deck. With a little push from Carl and a little pull from the crewman, she managed to complete the manoeuvre successfully, and sat down in the boat.

'Oh, it's really quite comfortable,' she said, surprised.

'Now, you're next,' said Mr Ismay, helping Mrs Latimer. Carl turned to Emilia. 'And then it will be your turn.'

'Very well. As long as you come too.'

'It's women and children first,' he reminded her.

'There were a number of gentlemen in the first boat. If there are not enough women and children to fill the second boat, then men will be allowed in, too.'

He frowned.

'I'm not going without you,' she said firmly.

'Very well,' he conceded. 'As long as there's room. If not, you're to go in the boat - no arguments - and I will get a later one.'

She saw the sense of this. 'Very well.'

He smiled. Then, putting his hands on her shoulders he drew her to him and kissed her on the forehead. She could feel the warmth of his body radiating outwards. If only they had been alone . . . Reluctantly he let her go.

'Oh!' Mrs Latimer let out a startled cry. She had almost fallen as a distress rocket, going off with a resounding boom, had taken her by surprise.

Carl gave her his attention, holding her beneath the elbow until she had successfully crossed to the small boat. Then he turned back to Emilia. Or, at least, back to where she had been.

'Emilia?' he said, looking round. Then, with a puzzled note in his voice, 'Emilia?'

His eyes scanned the boat deck. They roved over Colonel Astor's party, on past a group of ladies, then stopping and searching the group to make sure none of them were Emilia, before travelling across the deck to the lifeboat again. But he could not see her. He looked round again, more quickly this time, his eyes sweeping every group and scanning every face. He refused to accept what had happened, but as his eyes searched every last inch of deck around him, he had to face the truth.

Emilia had gone.

Nine

Emilia was watching Mrs Latimer climb into the lifeboat when she felt a hand clamp itself over her mouth from behind and she was dragged backwards, away from the boat, through the milling throng of people on the boat deck. She was so surprised that it was a minute before she could take in what was happening, let alone do anything about it, and the people she was dragged through were too intent on listening to the officers' orders to take an interest in one young woman who had nothing to do with them.

She was pulled from the boat deck to the promenade deck, by which time she had recovered from her shock enough to struggle. She began to hit and kick out with all her might. But it was to no avail. Her assailant cursed, but otherwise ignored her efforts to break free as he dragged her towards the lift.

She could not see who it was that had hold of her, as he – by his strength, she guessed it must be a man – was behind her. He dragged her into the lift, then his hand punched one of the buttons . . . and nothing happened.

The lights were still working, Emilia noticed, but when the ship had struck the iceberg, the power for the lifts must have gone out.

'Damn! The bloody lift's not working,' said her assailant. Her spirits sank. She recognized his voice. It was Barker.

Carl's man had been keeping an eye on him during the voyage, making sure he remained in steerage, but in all the confusion he must have managed to get away.

She renewed her struggles. She didn't know what Barker had to gain by seizing her at such a time, but he meant her no good, and the sooner she broke free the better.

He dragged her out of the lift again, his hand still clamped over her mouth, then pulled her kicking and struggling down the stairs.

If only someone would notice, she thought. But the sight of a woman struggling in the grip of a man was no longer noteworthy. Below decks, conditions had deteriorated. Stewards were no longer politely asking passengers to put on their life jackets and soothing them with reassurances that nothing was wrong. Instead they were pulling reluctant women from their staterooms and forcibly preventing them from returning, so that no one found it strange or objectionable to see a woman being treated so roughly.

How quickly things can change, thought Emilia. A few hours before, Barker would not have dared try such a thing, and if he had, he would have been immediately apprehended by the stewards. But he had dared it now. She must find a way out of the situation, because no one was going to help her. She would have to help herself.

Barker seemed to have no clear idea of what he was doing or where he was taking her. He pushed her in front of him, taking her whichever way seemed easiest, where the people were not so densely clustered. He eventually turned into one of the corridors leading to the cabins. They were, Emilia thought, in second class, although she could not be sure. She had lost her bearings in all the confusion. The narrow corridors all looked alike. If only she had taken more notice when she had visited second class before. But it was too late to think about that now.

The corridor was deserted. Some of the room doors were open. Some were closed. Far off, she heard one shut with a bang.

Apparently satisfied that the area was deserted, Barker pushed her into one of the empty rooms. As he did so she noticed the floor was not level; it had a slight slope downwards. But she had no time to think about it.

'What on earth do you think you're doing?' she demanded, as at last he let her go, throwing her across the room before closing the door. 'Mr Latimer will—'

'You and your Mr Latimer,' he spat. 'I've had enough of your Mr Latimer. Setting his man to watch me. Keeping tabs on me. Stopping me going about my business. So you'd better shut up about Mr Latimer if you don't want to feel the back of my hand.'

She eyed him warily, knowing he was capable of making good on his threat.

'I don't know what you think you'll gain by kidnapping me,' she said.

'A fortune, that's what. The ship's sinking. I'm just keeping my investment safe.'

'The ship isn't sinking,' she contradicted him. 'The lifeboats are being launched as a precaution. In an hour or two this will all be over and Carl will be wanting to know where I am.'

'Oh, it's sinking, all right. I heard Andrews telling the captain. And when it does, you and I are going to be safe. I'm going to take you to a nice little place I know of, a hide-away, in New York, where you'll stay until I've telegraphed Mr Montmorency and he's come to collect his wares. I would have sent a telegraph from the ship, but that blasted Hutton's dogged my every move. Still, never mind. I can telegraph from New York instead.'

Emilia was appalled. Although she had begun to suspect the situation was more serious than she had at first supposed, she had not actually believed *Titanic* was going to sink.

'If the ship's sinking, then you'll never get off, unless you take one of the lifeboats, and you can't hope to keep hold of me when we're in a boat. As soon as the rescue ship appears you'll lose me again. In the confusion of getting aboard, I'll slip away.'

'Oh, will you? Not if I knock you out, you won't. There'll be plenty of stuff in the infirmary for keeping you quiet.'

'And you don't think that will look suspicious?' she challenged him. 'Carrying an unconscious woman on to the boat?'

'No one will care. It's civilized enough at the moment, but I've come from steerage and the water down there's knee deep. Once everyone's realized the ship's going to sink there'll be a panic, and no one will care what I do or don't do with my *wife*. They'll be too busy worrying about their own skins to care about yours. But if, by any chance anyone asks, I'll tell them I gave my poor wife a sedative. There are a lot of hysterical women on board the ship right now, and no one will question the actions of a concerned husband who wanted to knock his wife out to keep her from panicking.'

'You'll never manage it,' said Emilia hotly.

'Oh. I'll manage it, all right, and a good deal more besides. When I get off this ship, I'm not only going to have you with me but I'm going to be rich besides. All the nobs are up on deck, either that or they've gone off in the boats, and they've left their money and jewels behind. The ship's ripe for looting. A man with a strong nerve can make a fortune out of something like this, and no one's got a stronger nerve than me. One way or another, I'm going to come out of this little trip a wealthy man. In fact, I might just be a millionaire. So you can shut up and sit down and keep out of my way.'

He pushed her into a chair and, drawing a couple of pieces of rope out of his pocket, he pulled her arms behind her, round the back of the chair. He wrapped the first piece of rope round her arms and chest, securing them to the chair as he did so, and tying the second rope round her feet, again tying them to the chair. She struggled, but he was too strong for her, and she was held fast.

She was tempted to scream for help, but she knew that no one would hear her. And even if they did, they would dismiss her as a hysterical woman who was screaming because of the situation. So she saved her energy, hoping she would be able to see a way out of her predicament before it was too late.

'Now, let's see what there is here,' he said, pulling out the drawers. He whistled. 'Look at all this!' He took out bundles of money and stuffed them into his pockets. His eyes were gleaming and he laughed loudly. 'And this is only the start.'

'You're a fool,' she said with contempt. 'If the ship's sinking, you haven't got time to waste.'

'I've got an hour or so. Andrews told the captain. That's plenty of time for me to do my thing. Now you stay here, like a good girl, and I'll go and see what else I can find.'

He went out, closing the door behind him.

An hour! Emilia's spirits plummeted. Was that all the time they had left? Although she had begun to think it possible the ship might sink, it was very different to hear that it was going to do so in such a short space of time.

She had to get free. And then she had to get off *Titanic* before Barker could find her and make good on his threat to sedate her.

She struggled against her bonds but they were too well tied and she couldn't even loosen them. They were cutting into her wrists, and the more she struggled, the deeper they bit.

She paused, and drew breath. Think, she told herself. If you can't undo the ropes, then you must cut them.

She looked round the room for something she could use. Her eyes alighted on a paper knife on a small table. It was lying tantalizingly near the edge.

She began to rock her chair, building up enough momentum to move it forwards in a shuffling movement. It was slow work, but gradually the desk drew nearer. She paused for breath when she reached it, then with great difficulty rocked her chair from side to side, manoeuvring it so that her back was to the desk. She tried to pick up the paper knife. At the third attempt she managed it. Allowing it to slip down through her hands, she brought the blade into contact with the bonds that tied her hands behind her back. But she could get no leverage, and besides, the knife was not sharp enough. It would not cut the rope.

Frustrated, she dropped it to the floor. She would have to think again. There must be some way of getting free. Her eyes ran round the room. Over in the corner she saw a washstand. On it was a cut-throat razor. Yes. That would cut the ropes. But it would also, if she was not careful, cut her wrists.

She hesitated. But in the end her desire to be free outweighed her fear. Repeating the rocking movement with her chair she managed to manoeuvre her way across to the washstand, where she began the difficult task of trying to pick up the razor. She failed at the first three attempts, but at the fourth one she finally managed it. She took a deep breath, then attempted to cut through the ropes.

It was working. She could feel the ropes give. And then the razor slipped, and cut the mound beneath her thumb.

She dropped the razor in shock and then cursed herself for doing so. Though her wound bled freely, it was not serious, and if she had not dropped the razor she would have been able to try again.

She closed her eyes in frustration, but she had no time to indulge in recriminations. She must find another way to free herself.

She looked round the stateroom again but there was nothing she could use to help her. No more knives or razors. Nothing sharp. Just beds and tables and chairs. All useless.

She felt her spirits plummet still further. If she could not manage to free herself, she would be at Barker's mercy. And mercy was a quality Barker did not possess.

Up on deck, Carl was becoming worried. He had not been too anxious at first, assuming Emilia must just have slipped out of sight but with every passing minute he was growing more concerned. Although it did not seem possible, Emilia had vanished. What made matters worse was that the scene was beginning to become ugly. The disbelief of half an hour before was starting to turn to fear as the ship began to tilt forward, and people began to realize there was a serious possibility *Titanic* could sink. He must find Emilia, and find her quickly, if he was going to be able to get her into a boat.

His mother's boat had left almost half an hour ago. It had not waited for Emilia, but had been lowered to the water with its small group of passengers and then rowed away from the ship. Still, there were other boats. All he had to do was find Emilia.

He left the starboard deck, which he had already searched, and went round to the port side. Most of the lifeboats had gone.

Standing by one of them he saw Mr and Mrs Thirske. He went over to them.

'Have you seen Miss Cavendish?' he shouted, trying to make himself heard over the loud boom of the distress rockets, which were being launched into the sky at regular intervals.

'No, I'm sorry, I haven't,' said Mrs Thirske. 'Isn't this terrible? Do you think the ship will really go down?'

His face was grim. 'I think it likely,' he said.

'Perhaps Miss Cavendish has gone back to her stateroom,' suggested Mr Thirske. 'Did she need a coat?'

'No, she was warmly dressed.'

'Still, you know what women are. One of the ladies on board wanted to take her lucky pig. Perhaps Miss Cavendish has gone to get a mascot.'

'Thank you. Yes, perhaps she has.'

He didn't think it likely, but he had searched the deck and she wasn't there, so he decided he had nothing to lose by trying her stateroom. It was a small chance he would find her there, but the only one he had. He fought his way through a mass of people coming the other way, but once in the first-class corridors, it was deserted. Doors were flung open, revealing magnificent interiors in a state of disarray. Beds had been abandoned with their pillows rumpled and covers thrown back. Drawers were open where passengers had hastily retrieved their belongings, or where looters had been at work.

It brought the enormity of the situation home to him. The beautiful ship, the pride of the White Star Line, with its elegant staterooms, its cafés and libraries, its squash courts and Turkish baths, would perish. And all the souls on board, if they did not manage to get into the lifeboats, would perish with it.

He hurried now, running along the corridor to Emilia's state-room as the ship shifted beneath his feet. The tilt was becoming more pronounced, with the bow sinking ever lower and the stern rising higher, so that it was difficult to make progress.

At last he reached her stateroom. He flung the door wide, but she was not inside. He went though the sitting room to the bedroom, then tried the second bedroom before going out on to her covered deck. But she was nowhere to be found. Moreover, it did not look as though she had been back to her stateroom since collecting her coat. There was no sign of haste or confusion. Everything was neat and tidy, apart from the blocks of ice, almost completely melted, over by the porthole.

He ran his hand through his hair, wondering what to do next. And then a cold feeling gripped him. What if Barker had eluded Hutton's watchful eye? In all the confusion it was only too likely.

But then why had Hutton not come to tell him? Because he was trying to find Barker, Carl guessed. But where would Barker take her? Steerage? It was certainly where his room was placed. But would he have returned there with the ship sinking, given that the steerage accommodation was on the lower decks?

There was only one way to find out.

He went down to the second-class accommodation, scarcely noticing the water that crept over his shoes and then swirled around his ankles, but when he reached steerage it was too deep and cold to be ignored.

'Damn!' he cursed.

Still he went on, wading through the icy water, calling as he did so. 'Emilia? Emilia!'

But there was no reply.

Emilia made another effort to break free of her bonds. She twisted her wrists in an effort to loosen the ropes, but to no avail. Even worse, the ropes grated over her cut and made it bleed more. But she had to get free. It had been bad enough before, but since the ship had shifted, water had started to creep under the door. If she did not release herself soon she would drown.

She was just making another effort to work the ropes loose when the door opened and a woman – a maidservant by the look of her – entered the stateroom. She was dressed in a coat and wide-brimmed hat. A shawl was wrapped round her neck and shoulders.

Emilia felt a wave of relief. She was saved!

'Oh, thank goodness,' she said. 'You have to help me. There's a man, he kidnapped me and tied me up. I have to get away before he. . .' Her voice trailed away as she saw the woman more clearly. It was not a woman at all. It was Barker, dressed in women's clothes.

'No need to look so surprised,' he sneered. 'I haven't gone mad. I'm just taking a few precautions, that's all. They're sticking to women and children first up there. Trouble is, there aren't enough boats to go round, which means that anyone left 'til the end – the men – won't be getting off at all. But I'm not going down with the ship. I wanted to get something from the ship's infirmary to keep you quiet, but there wasn't time, so I'll have to make do with this.'

He pulled something out of the pocket in his skirt. It was a revolver.

'Plenty of these lying around,' he smirked. 'Plenty of everything, just there for the taking. Money, stocks, bonds, jewels – paradise. A shame I didn't have longer. Still . . .' He jangled his pockets. 'Can't complain. But if you're thinking of making a fuss,' he said, waving the gun threateningly, 'you'd better think again.'

'It seems like I have no choice.'

Emilia appeared to be docile. It had occurred to her that, when Barker untied her bonds, he would have to put down the gun. That would be the moment for her to make an attempt to escape. So if he thought she had given in, so much the better.

'That's it. You be a good girl and I'll get you out of this.'

He tucked the gun in the top of his skirt, then went round behind her to untie her ropes.

This was her chance.

As soon as her hands and feet were loose she stood up and spun round, making an effort to grasp the gun. But he was too quick for her.

'Oh, no, you don't,' he said, grabbing her wrist with one hand, whilst he retrieved the gun with the other. 'There's no way I'm letting you get hold of that.'

He jerked her round and pushed her in front of him, facing forwards, twisting her arm up behind her to keep her compliant. Then he pushed her out of the room and down the corridor. She could do nothing about it: he was holding the gun to the small of her back. Propelling her forward, he pushed her through the corridors and finally up on to the deck.

Emilia gasped. She had expected to see a similar scene to the one she had left behind, with people stepping into the lifeboats in an orderly fashion, but it was like something out of a nightmare. There was no order or discipline, and the smell of fear was in the air. Officers were waving revolvers as they guarded the lifeboats against groups of men who looked as though they could rush them at minute, whilst women climbed on board. As she watched in horror, one of the officers fired a couple of warning shots over the men's heads. Women were no longer being coaxed into the boats. Those who would not go of their own accord were being picked up and thrown in bodily.

Ropes creaked. Rockets boomed. It was like a scene from hell.

'My God,' said Barker.

Emilia stood, frozen with horror. But by and by her wits began to return. Despite the growing terror all around her, she was relieved to be out on deck. At least now she had a chance of escape – as long as Barker lowered the gun, that was.

But his hand did not waver, and he kept it pressed to her back.

'Over there,' he said, indicating a place further down the deck where a lifeboat was being loaded.

Emilia had no choice but to go where the gun prompted her to go. The crowds around the boats were getting unruly. The officers were shouting and swearing at the men to get back whilst the women got into the boats. She knew the time was fast approaching when she must try and make good her escape. Once in a boat with Barker she would be lost. He had only to knock her out with a well-placed blow, and in the confusion it would not be seen. Then he would be able to carry her, unconscious, on to the rescue ship – if a rescue ship arrived – and she would be in his power.

He pushed her over to one of the lifeboats.

'Women and children,' called the officers. 'Are there any more women and children? Come on, miss,' said one, grabbing her arm and pulling her into the boat.

As she started to fall into the boat, the gun was no longer

at her back. It was her chance. As soon as her foot hit the seat of the lifeboat she twisted round and ripped the hat from Barker's head. Without its shadow, he was revealed for the man he was. It was enough to make him hesitate for a minute. Then, recovering himself, he waved the gun, but behind him, an officer cracked a revolver down hard on his head. He swayed, and toppled, and fell between the lifeboat and the side of the ship . . . straight into the icy waters below. In his haste to loot the staterooms he had not put on a life jacket. With the weight of the guns, to say nothing of the stolen gems in his pockets, Emilia knew he would go straight to the bottom.

'Lower away!' came the cry.

It brought her thoughts back to the present.

The ropes creaked, the davits groaned, and the boat began its descent towards the sea. But she did not want to leave the ship in a lifeboat. Not without Carl.

Acting quickly, she launched herself at the side of the ship. She managed to find a hand hold on one of the lower rails and began to pull herself back on to deck, but her thumb was still bleeding, and her wrists were sore from where they had been tied, and to her horror, she felt her grip starting to slip. If she slipped she would fall, down, down to the ocean, exactly as Barker had done, to die of cold in the icy waters or to be crushed between the unsteadily lowering lifeboat and the ship.

She redoubled her efforts, trying desperately to renew her handhold. She had a firm hold with her left hand but had to fight for purchase with her right. It was wet with blood where her cut had opened up and her fingers kept slipping. She swung herself from her left hand, trying to build up enough momentum to hook her right elbow over the lower rail, but the fingers on her left hand were starting to open with the strain. She closed them, gritting her teeth against the pain.

And then she was aware of strong hands reaching down, catching her under her arms and lifting her up and out of danger. As her foot drew level with the rail she pushed against it, giving an added impetus to her rescue. She was being lifted over the rail, and as she was lowered to the deck and her eyes drew level with her rescuer, she felt her heart leap before a warm feeling flooded her whole being.

'Carl!'

Her eyes met his, and the relief she saw there made her spirits soar.

He lowered her gently until her feet touched the deck, but even when she was standing safely in front of him he did not let her go. His eyes ran over her face and body, drinking her in.

'Emilia,' he said. His hand cupped her cheek.

And then he dragged her into his arms and kissed her with all the fire of his being and she returned his kisses with equal fervour. They were both of them lost in their joy of having found each other, and it blotted out the nightmare all around them, until at last he let her go.

'Emilia!' he said. 'I've been so worried. What happened? Where did you go?

'It was Barker,' she told him. 'He must have eluded Hutton. He dragged me down to a cabin and tied me up whilst he looted the ship. I tried to escape, but it was impossible. He'd dressed up as a woman to get on to the same life boat as me, and I had only one chance to reveal him as a man when he tried to climb aboard the boat with me.'

'Thank God it worked,' said Carl.

'And thank goodness you were there to save me,' she said. She shuddered. 'When my fingers started slipping, I thought I was going to fall.'

He took her hands and raised them to his lips, kissing them fervently. Then he noticed the mound beneath her thumb.

'You're bleeding,' he said.

'I tried to cut my ropes with a razor. I cut myself instead.'

He pulled a large handkerchief out of his pocket and pressed it tightly over the cut. Then, when the blood stopped flowing, he removed it in order to tear off a strip with which to bind the handkerchief pad in place.

'It really ought to be cleaned, but there's no time,' he said. 'I have to get you off the ship.'

There was a serious tilt to the deck now. It seemed to be

slipping away beneath their feet. The stern was rising out of the water as the bow sank ever deeper, dragged down by the weight of water it had taken on board.

As far as Emilia could see, all the boats on the starboard side of the ship had gone.

'Come on, we'll try the port side,' said Carl.

Catching Emilia by the hand, he rushed with her round to the other side of the ship.

In her haste, Emilia tripped and saw that she had almost fallen over piles of bread on the deck. Bread? she thought in surprise, before realizing it must be meant to supply the lifeboats. But by the size of the piles, although the bread had been carried on to the deck, none of it had gone any further.

Even if they could find a lifeboat, how would they manage to stay alive until help reached them? Was it hours away? Days away? Would it ever come? She did not know. But she would worry about that later. Right now, she needed to get to a boat.

She and Carl reached the port side of the ship, close to the stern. There was a boat being loaded.

'This is it,' Carl said, turning her towards him. 'This is your boat.'

A cry of 'Women and children only,' rang out in the night.

'No. I'm not going unless you go,' she said.

'Yes, you are. You are going to do exactly as I tell you. You are going to get in that boat, if I have to lift you in myself.'

'No,' she said resolutely.

'If you think I'm going to let you drown, you're mistaken,' he said, taking her face between his hands and looking deep into her eyes.

'Carl, there aren't enough lifeboats for everyone,' she said.

'I'm not going without you.'

'Now listen to me. You're right, there aren't enough lifeboats to go round, but the wireless operators have managed to get off a number of distress calls and the *Olympic*'s coming to rescue us. She'll be here soon. If I don't get off in a boat, I'll get off some other way. There are tables, chairs – all things that float.'

'But the water's so cold,' she protested.

'It doesn't matter. It's calm – thank God it's not a stormy night. I'm strong, and a good swimmer, and if you think I'm going to drown just when I've met the woman I love then you're mistaken. Now get into the boat.'

'Love?' she asked.

'Yes. Love. I love you, Emilia. Which is why I'm going to put you on a boat and why you are going to get in it. Because once I know you're safe, I can put all my thoughts, my time and my energy into saving myself.'

She didn't like it. She hated it. The thought of losing Carl was too terrible to contemplate. But she knew that what he said was true. If she went into the water with him, she would only be a burden. She could not swim very well, and he would have to expend much of his precious energy on helping her. Whereas if she was safely in a boat, he could save himself. Reluctantly she agreed.

'Thank you.'

He kissed her softly. All his love went into the kiss, all his tenderness and affection, and she never wanted it to end. But it had to end.

He took her over to the boat, which had already been lowered, and was now almost at the water.

'Damn!' he cursed.

Emilia looked down. The water had risen, and was now no more than twenty feet below the deck. She could not help remembering the time when the seaman had tried to test the water temperature – was it really only that morning? No, it was yesterday morning, for it was after midnight now and so of course it was Monday. Even so, less than twenty-four hours before the water had been seventy-five feet beneath the deck. Now it was twenty feet below. How soon before it would be ten feet below? Then five . . . ?

She turned her attention back to the deck. Things were degenerating still further. Though the orchestra played, there was an atmosphere of panic. Women were being thrown into boats. There were shouts of 'aft' and 'stern' as the lifeboats were lowered, and the crew called to each other to communicate which end of the boat needed lowering next. Though the boats were meant to be lowered level, there was now so much confusion it was lucky they were being lowered at all. The second they hit the water they were being rowed away from the ship.

'Get away!' the officers were instructing the men in the boats. 'Row right away, or you'll be caught in the suction when the ship goes down.'

'Come on,' said Carl, 'there might be more boats at the front of the ship. There are two collapsible boats tethered to the roof of the officers' quarters above the boat deck, I know. They haven't been launched yet.'

They raced down to the other end of the ship, just missing another boat. But the collapsibles were being slid down planks on to the deck. With the deck itself being now nearly under water, people were throwing chairs and tables into the water, anything that could float. Others were making their way up to the stern. It was rising further and further out of the water. The ship was at an angle of forty-five degrees, and the angle was steepening every minute. Priests were giving the last rites as they hung on to railings to prevent themselves from sliding down the decks. The ship creaked and groaned under the terrific strain. And through it all, the orchestra played on.

Emilia marvelled at their courage. They had made no attempt to save themselves, but had kept panic at bay until almost the last moment with their lively music. Even now, they were creating an oasis of calm in the middle of the madness. The music had changed, though. Instead of cheerful ragtime tunes they were playing a hymn. She began to hum without realizing it. It was '*Nearer my God to Thee*'.

As she and Carl drew near the bridge, she saw Captain Smith with a megaphone in his hand. Perspiration was running down his face as he continued to give orders, doing what he could to save the remaining souls on his doomed ship.

The stern rose further in the air. People were running up

the deck in an effort to reach the top, pushing past Emilia and Carl, who were running the other way. The remaining lifeboats, if they could be released from their place on top of the officers' quarters, were downwards towards the encroaching sea. The ship was sinking deeper and deeper with every minute, and water was creeping up the deck, but still, the boats at the front offered the best chance of escape.

'Do your best for the women and children,' called the captain to his crew. 'Then look after yourselves.'

He himself made no move towards the last of the boats. He didn't throw anything in the water. He stayed on the bridge. Emilia saw his eyes, and with a feeling of fatality she knew he meant to go down with the ship.

The collapsible lifeboat had now been pulled down on to the deck.

'Get in,' said Carl.

Emilia needed no second bidding. The deck was awash. The water was around her knees, and was rising steadily. She lifted one foot from the deck, but a wave caught her and knocked her away. Carl grasped her around the waist and lifted her in. She landed in water which had washed over the side, but she was lucky to be in a boat.

'And you,' she said, reaching out a hand to him.

He glanced along the deck. There were no more women and children in sight, no one else who could be saved. He nodded. He lifted his foot in order to climb in, and then another wave knocked him off his feet, and swept him away.

'No!'

She tried to climb out of the boat after him, but strong hands pulled her back.

'He's gone,' a man's voice said.

'No!'

She fought against them, trying to break free, but at last she stilled. There was no more sign of Carl. Even if she left the boat, she would not be able to find him. But then she told herself not to despair. Swept from the ship he might have been, but he was strong, and a good swimmer. He had said so himself. He had been wearing a life jacket and he knew to swim away from the ship before the suction pulled him under.

He was alive. He would make it through somehow.

She clung on to that hope. Because hope was all she had.

Ten

The boat pulled away from the ship. *Titanic*'s bow was rapidly going down and the stern was rising higher and higher out of the water. People were sliding down the decks or being thrown into the water. The air was filled with screaming. Emilia blotted it all out. The screams weren't Carl's. They couldn't be Carl's. He must be safe. Anything else was too terrible to contemplate.

The lights were still burning and the orchestra still playing as the lifeboat pulled further and further away from the ship. On board, she could see people still struggling to climb the sloping deck, but even if they reached the highest point, she knew they would not be safe. Nothing could save *Titanic* now, even though the lights were still burning and the orchestra playing. It was doomed.

Then suddenly the lights went out.

It was a shock to see the brilliant ship grow suddenly dark. It was like a foreshadowing of the end. The ship was now no more than a black silhouette against the sky. Its propellers rose further and further out of the water as the bow of the ship went further and further down.

And then there was a terrible roar, and millions of sparks shot into the sky.

'That's the boilers,' said one of the seamen on the boat. 'They've come lose and fallen through the bulkheads.'

There were two more explosions, seemingly below the surface of the water, and then with a huge groan the ship began to break in two. Emilia looked on in horror as *Titanic* split between the third and fourth funnels, right down to the keel. The bow plunged forwards and downwards, disappearing beneath the waves. But the stern, free of the huge weight of the submerged bow, righted itself, and bobbed on the water. For a minute it looked as though it was going to float.

Emilia held her breath. The funnel broke loose and toppled. Then the stern began to sink, too.

'She's still attached to the bow at the keel,' said one of the seamen.

The stern, pulled down by the bow, began to sink at the front and rise at the back. It was gradual to begin with, but then ever more rapid. The angle steepened and the propellers rose higher and higher into the air. Up and up, until the stern was vertical. It stood there for a moment, a mountain against the sky, and then slid majestically into the water, straight down, until it had disappeared.

There was a terrible silence aboard the lifeboat.

'She's gone,' one of the seamen breathed.

There was nothing more to see. Darkness hid the struggles of those in the water, but nothing could hide their cries. They were dreadful.

'We have to go back,' said Emilia.

'We can't.'

'We must,' she protested. 'Those people will die if we don't help them.'

'We can't do it,' said one of the seamen. 'If we do we'll be pulled under. The ship's creating suction as she sinks. We have to wait. Then we can go back.'

Emilia acknowledged the truth of this. Even so, she strained her eyes, trying to see if any of the vague shapes struggling in the water was Carl, and hoping against hope that he was alive.

Other lifeboats were rowing about nearby. There was a green light in one of them. It was a great help in keeping the boats together, for although there were stars, there was no moon and the night was black.

It seemed an eternity before anything could be done to help the poor souls in the water. Far off, Emilia could see a group of boats. They were floating so close to each other that she wondered whether they had been tied together. And then, at last, one of the boats from the group started to row back towards *Titanic*.

She sat up straight. 'Now it's time for us to go back, too,' she said.

'Not bloody likely,' said one of the men in the boat. 'We'll be swamped. We're staying where we are.'

She rounded on him. 'Can't you hear the cries? Those people are dying. The man I love is amongst them. We're going back.'

She picked up an oar but it was wrenched out of her hands.

'Are you really going to sit by and do nothing whilst those people freeze to death?'

'Better them than us,' muttered another man.

The mood in the boat was becoming hostile.

'Don't mind her,' said a woman, putting an arm round her. 'She's just upset. She'll soon settle down.'

Emilia bit her lip. She knew what the woman was doing. She was trying to protect her from the fear and guilt of the other people in the lifeboat, which was in danger of turning into violence.

'There, there, dearie, never you mind,' went on the woman. 'One of the other boats is going back, look. Maybe they'll rescue your man.'

Emilia nodded. Maybe it would. It had to. She loved Carl. She couldn't lose him. But she could do nothing to help him.

It was a weary time in the boat. No one knew for sure if the distress signals had been seen. There was talk of another ship, supposedly sighted not far away even as *Titanic* was sinking, but there was no sign of it, and this led the people in Emilia's boat to doubt the other reassuring stories they had heard.

'I heard the *Baltic* was coming,' said one of the women. 'The steward told me quite clearly the *Baltic* had been summoned and was on her way.'

'No, the *Olympic*,' said another. 'She'll be here this afternoon.'

'I heard it was the *Carpathia*,' said a man.

'I wish they'd hurry, whoever they are,' said one of the women pathetically. 'My feet are so cold.'

There was water in the bottom of the boat, and it was icy.
'And there are no supplies,' said one of the men. 'If we're
adrift for any length of time we won't survive.'

Emilia thought of the piles of bread she had tripped over
on the deck. They had never been put aboard the boats. She
remembered Pansy saying there was usually a lifeboat drill
on the first Sunday of a voyage. Why Captain Smith had
decided not to hold one on this voyage she did not know, but
it had left the passengers and crew ill prepared for an emergency. The boats had been lowered slowly and only half filled.
There had been no provisions put on board. Passengers had
not known where to go or what to do. Still, it was too late to
worry about it now. *Titanic* had gone. Captain Smith had
gone. She shuddered as she thought of the last view she had
had of him, being washed off the bridge by a wave.

'Perhaps they just told us there was a ship coming to reassure us,' said one of the women, voicing everyone's fears.
'Perhaps no one's coming for us. Perhaps we'll float here
without food or water for days. Perhaps we'll never be found.
Perhaps—'

'The *Olympic*'s coming,' said Emilia firmly, hearing the
rising panic in the woman's voice. 'I heard the captain tell
the First Officer that the *Olympic* was on her way. He might
lie to the passengers to reassure them, but he wouldn't lie to
the officers.'

She had not heard him say any such thing, but she knew
it was vital to keep up everyone's spirits. Out in the middle
of the ocean, in the freezing cold, with icebergs all around
them, if they did not keep up their spirits, they would not
survive.

'True,' murmured one of the men. 'He wouldn't lie to a
fellow officer.'

'What would be the point?' agreed another.

The panic began to subside. It was replaced by a despon-
dent air. They were adrift in the Atlantic, miles from land.
They were cold and wet and frightened. They could do nothing
to help themselves. Now all they could do was wait.

It was a long night. But after what seemed like an age, the

day at last began to dawn. As the sun streaked the horizon with shades of red and gold, Emilia began to feel renewed hope. Although the view was desolate, it had a beauty all its own. Everywhere she looked there was ice. Huge chunks of it floated on the surface of the vast ocean, coloured in shades of red and pink and yellow by the early morning sun. In the distance was the towering iceberg that had sunk *Titanic*. It looked peaceful, serenely unaware of the damage it had wrought. Its craggy slopes glowed in the sunshine, sparkling like diamonds where the facets caught the light.

Beyond the ice there was nothing. Not a scrap of land in sight. There was nothing but the ocean and the great mass of ice. And, despite the beauty, they were afloat without food or water, and numb with cold.

The boat began to rock gently. At first she found the movement soothing, but then realized that the sea was starting to grow rough. It had been calm overnight, as flat as a piece of glass, without a breath of wind to stir it. But now waves were starting to appear, and they were growing bigger. The fragile boats could not last in the open if the weather should turn.

There was no conversation. Everyone in the boat was too tired and too worn out by the events of the night to speak. But presently one of the woman facing Emilia broke her silence. 'A ship.' She spoke with rising joy. 'Look! Over there. It's a ship.'

Emilia hardly dared turn round. At last she did so, slowly, and saw a wonderful sight. There, coming towards them, was the unmistakeable black and red stack of a ship.

'We're saved!'

The cry ran round the little boat.

But then the ship stopped.

'What's she doing?' asked one of the men. 'Hasn't she seen us?'

'She can't get any closer because of all the floating ice,' said one of the seamen. 'We'll have to go to her. Pull those oars.'

Men and women both took hold of the oars and began to pull with all their might.

'It's *Carpathia*,' said one of the seamen as they drew closer. Emilia pulled her oar with renewed strength. Slowly but surely the small boat neared *Carpathia*. It was not the only one. There were other boats approaching the ship. They came from all directions, carrying the survivors of *Titanic*. Perhaps Carl was amongst them, Emilia thought.

She pulled on her oar, as her spirits began to rise.

The boat drew closer still to *Carpathia*. She could see figures now, climbing up the side of the ship from one of the lifeboats which had drawn up alongside. They were climbing up a rope ladder which had been let down from *Carpathia*. Next to them were figures being hauled on to the ship by way of a bosun's chair. Mail sacks, too, were going up and down. To begin with, she didn't trust her eyesight, but then she realized what the mail sacks were for. Babies were being put into them so that they could be pulled on board.

The light continued to grow, and with a last heave of the oars, Emilia's boat reached the side of the ship. She let go of her oar with relief. Her arms were aching, and her back felt like it was breaking. Her palms were blistered and the wound beneath her thumb had started to bleed again. But none of it mattered. She had reached *Carpathia*. She was safe.

Even now, some of the other survivors from her boat were climbing up the rope ladder. She stood up and reached out to take hold of it, but her hands were so numb she could not grip it. She tried again.

'Here,' said one of the seamen in her boat. 'Take the bosun's chair.'

It had been lowered again. Emilia sat on the seat and held on to the ropes as best she could, then with a jolt the chair began to rise. The sea grew further and further away from her as she was pulled up to *Carpathia*, and at last she was safely aboard. A blanket was wrapped round her shoulders and someone put a flask into her hand.

'Drink this.'

She took a sip, and spluttered. It was brandy.

'And again,' the voice said.

She took another sip.

The brandy was like fire in her mouth, but it quickly began to warm her through. It put some life back into her, and although she was exhausted she was able to move.

'There's a hot meal waiting for you downstairs,' said one of *Carpathia*'s officers.

'I have to find Carl,' she said, turning to him entreatingly. 'Do you know if he's been brought aboard? Mr Carl Latimer.'

'I can't tell you,' said the officer sympathetically. 'We've a lot of *Titanic*'s survivors on board, and more boats are coming in. I don't know if Mr Latimer's amongst them. But there's a hot meal waiting for you downstairs.'

'Later,' said Emilia.

She could not eat, could not think, until she knew if Carl was alive. She handed the flask back to him and then, ignoring his kind remarks about a hot meal, she went round the deck looking for Carl. There were many survivors on board, all bearing signs of shock, but Carl was not among them. She went over to the rail. More boats were coming in all the time. Carl, she told herself, would be in one of them.

She refused to face the possibility that he might not have survived.

Eleven

M rs Gisborne was sitting in one of the first-class state-rooms on *Carpathia* sipping a cup of tea. To look at her, no one would have guessed she had just been involved in a terrible disaster. She was immaculately dressed in an Empire-line gown with smart, low-heeled shoes. Her hair was artistically arranged in an elaborate, loose chignon, and she was calm and composed.

She sipped her tea delicately then put her cup back into the saucer.

'It must have been dreadful for you,' said Patricia Braithwaite sympathetically.

Mrs Braithwaite was one of Mrs Gisborne's society friends. She was a statuesque woman with black hair and blue eyes, and was dressed in the latest fashion. She had been travelling on *Carpathia* when news of the disaster had reached Captain Rostron. The captain had immediately turned the ship around and set out for *Titanic*'s last known coordinates. Knowing that Mrs Gisborne was on board, Mrs Braithwaite had awaited her friend on the deck, and had taken her to her stateroom as soon as she had boarded the ship.

With them was Dolly Frampton, another of their society friends, a graceful woman with red hair who had been travelling aboard *Carpathia* with Mr and Mrs Braithwaite. They were sitting clustered around a console table on which was a silver tray with a pot of tea with three cups and saucers. A plate of biscuits was next to it.

'It was awful,' Mrs Gisborne agreed.

Despite the tragedy, she was in remarkably good spirits. She had been in one of the early boats to escape *Titanic*, and

157

had avoided the scenes of panic that had become prevalent later when it became clear that the ship was going to sink. She had been warmly dressed, and had even had a blanket for her knees, so that she had suffered none of the terrible exposure of other passengers. There had been plenty of seamen aboard her boat, so that she had not had to row, and in addition, her husband's flask of spirits had kept out the worst of the cold. Not even the cries of the drowning had shaken her for long. She had never empathized with other people's sorrows, and had congratulated herself on escaping the disaster rather than feeling for those who had not been so lucky.

'How terrible to lose everything. I don't know what I'd do if my jewels were at the bottom of the sea,' said Dolly, fingering her pearl necklace.

Mrs Gisborne arranged her shawl around her shoulders. The shawl was her only concession to the fact that she had spent the night in a lifeboat instead of a warm stateroom, and was now feeling a little chilled.

'Fortunately, we took everything of value with us,' she said. 'I heard the captain talking to Mr Andrews just after the ship hit the iceberg. Mr Andrews said the ship would sink. I didn't believe it at first, but when I saw his eyes I knew it was true. I alerted Thomas and we returned to our stateroom, putting on an extra layer of clothing and collecting our valuables. Janice picked up blankets for our knees and pillows for us to sit on, and we made our way back to the deck. We left in one of the first boats.'

'There must have been a terrible rush for the boats,' said Mrs Frampton.

'Not at all. No one wanted to get in. The crew told everyone there was no danger, and no one believed the ship would sink.'

'So that's why your boat was only half full,' said Mrs Braithwaite. 'And why it had so many gentlemen.'

Mrs Gisborne nodded. 'It was women and children first, of course, but once there were no more women and children in sight – or at least, no more who would get in – the gentlemen were allowed to embark.' She frowned. 'The thing I am vexed

158

about is that Carl Latimer did not get in a boat. I saw him on deck with that little kitchen maid, but he went below for his mother and I never saw him again. I only hope he caught a later boat.'

'No, he didn't,' said Mrs Braithwaite.

'No?' Mrs Gisborne sighed heavily. 'Then it is the ruination of all my plans, and the ruination of Isabelle.'

'Not necessarily,' said Mrs Braithwaite. 'Although he didn't manage to climb aboard a boat, he was pulled out of the sea after *Titanic* went down. He'd been in the water a long time. I saw him brought on board *Carpathia*. He was unconscious, but alive.'

Mrs Gisborne's face cleared. 'Thank goodness,' she said.

'Of course, he may not live,' said Mrs Braithwaite.

'Oh, he'll live. He's a fighter. He clawed his way up from poverty to be a millionaire. Men like that don't lay down and die. Where is he now?'

'His mother is taking care of him. She came aboard shortly after he did and saw him on the deck. Mr Donaldson, one of Carl's business associates, gave them his stateroom.'

Mrs Gisborne gave a satisfied smile. 'Then all is well.'

'Are he and Isabelle engaged yet?' asked Mrs Frampton.

'Not yet,' said Mrs Gisborne, 'but they will be.' She frowned. 'As long as that little upstart didn't survive.'

'You mentioned her before,' said Dolly curiously. 'A kitchen maid you called her. Who is she?'

'A common little nobody. A goddaughter of one of Charlotte's school friends – oh, not one of our kind, I assure you. She was only able to travel on *Titanic* thanks to Charlotte's generosity, and was a laughing stock on board. You'll never believe it, but she wore a home-made dress in the first-class dining room.'

'Shocking,' murmured Mrs Frampton, wrinkling her nose.

'Unfortunately, as chance would have it, she attracted Carl's attention.'

'He doesn't seem the sort to take a fancy to a lame duck,' said Mrs Braithwaite, helping herself to a biscuit from the plate in the centre of the table and nibbling it delicately.

'Well, on this occasion, he did. And more than a fancy. I think he fell in love with her.'

Mrs Frampton and Mrs Braithwaite exchanged glances.

'Fortunately, *Titanic* sank, and with luck the problem of Miss Cavendish will have resolved itself.'

The ladies finished their tea, then Mrs Gisborne expressed her intention of visiting Carl. 'Where is the Donaldsons' stateroom?'

'I'll show you,' said Mrs Frampton. 'I want to call in and see how Carl is faring myself.'

They took their leave of Mrs Braithwaite.

'I think I will just go on deck for a minute and see if any of our other friends survived,' said Mrs Gisborne. 'The de Bretts were on board and I didn't see them leave the ship. It will be a terrible tragedy if they have perished. They were to hold a charity ball next month, and I have the most splendid gown to wear.'

The two ladies went up on to the deck. They paid no attention to the other survivors on deck but went across the deck towards the captain. If a list of survivors had been made, he would be the person who would know where it was.

They had almost reached him when Mrs Gisborne stopped.

'What is it?' asked Mrs Frampton. 'Have you seen the de Bretts?'

'No, more's the pity. It's not the de Bretts. It's *her.*'

Mrs Frampton followed her eyes to a young woman standing by the rail wrapped in a blanket.

'Out of all the people to survive, why did one of them have to be Emilia Cavendish?' said Mrs Gisborne in disgust. 'This could be the end of all our plans for Isabelle. If Carl survives, and he and Emilia find each other here, the ordeal they've been through will bring them together and they'll be engaged by the time they reach New York.' She thought. 'There's nothing for it, Dolly. You'll have to take her in.'

'Me?' asked Mrs Frampton in surprise.

'Yes, you. It's the only way we can keep the two of them apart. As long as you take her in, you can keep her in your stateroom so that she cannot go looking for him.'

'But won't *he* look for her?' asked Dolly. 'Even if I can

keep her below deck until we get back to New York, he will see her name on the survivors' list – the officers are drawing one up now. As soon as he does so he'll know she's on board, and sooner or later he will find her.'

'If he recovers sufficiently to look. Remember, he has been through a terrible ordeal and was unconscious when he was brought on board.'

'He has only to ask his mother to look for her, even if he is too weak to look himself, and he will find her.'

Mrs Gisborne thought. 'Then we must make sure we keep her name off the survivors' list. Let's just hope she hasn't already given it to one of the crew, though, judging by the condition she's in, it doesn't seem likely. Once she's in your stateroom we can give it for her, saying she's called Miss . . . Elsie Carter.'

'It won't work,' said Mrs Frampton regretfully. 'She will look for him.'

'She evidently doesn't know he's aboard, or she would not be standing by the railing. If we can get her below quickly enough we can prevent her hearing anything of him, and as for the survivor list, well, we will just have to find a way of keeping her away from it. But that is a problem for later. Now, we have to get her off the deck.' She thought. 'She had better not see me. I have already tried to warn her away from Carl and she might suspect something.'

'Very well. Leave it to me. In fact, if you would send my maid to me, I have an idea as to how I can get Miss Cavendish to abandon her vigil.'

Mrs Gisborne looked at her enquiringly.

'I will induce her to leave the deck by telling her that my maid will watch for her loved one in her place. I rely on you to tell Mary what's expected of her before you let her come on to the deck. Make sure she understands that under no circumstances is she to find him.'

'A good idea,' said Margaret approvingly. 'I can't thank you enough Dolly.'

Dolly smiled. 'My dear Margaret, what are friends for? Just make sure you invite me to the wedding.'

*   *   *

Emilia was weak and shivering. She had been given brandy on first boarding *Carpathia*, but had resisted the efforts of the crew to persuade her to go below and have a hot breakfast. She was sick with worry. She had failed to find Carl on deck, and she had gone over to the rail to watch further boats arriving. With each new boat that reached *Carpathia* her hopes rose, only to be dashed again when he was not on board. Now she was close to exhaustion.

Everywhere around her were the cries of distressed people, which lowered her spirits still more. So many people had lost loved ones, and with each new boat that arrived, bringing no sign of Carl, she feared she could be among them.

She had seen many people she knew brought on board: stewards and stewardesses; Mr and Mrs Thirske; and the waiter who had served her in the first-class dining room on her first night aboard *Titanic*. She had also seen Mr Ismay. The sight of him had shocked her. She had caught a glimpse of him as one of the lifeboats had drawn up alongside *Carpathia*. His face had been blue, and he had been staring ahead of him, like a statue.

'I should have gone down with the ship,' she had heard him saying as he had come aboard. 'Women went down. I should have.'

One of the men in her boat had seen Mr Ismay leave the ship. He had not left until all the wooden boats had been launched on the starboard side of the ship. Only the collapsible boats had remained. He himself had left in one of the collapsible boats, and he had only done so after the crew had ensured him there were no more women and children in the vicinity. But still, he had survived.

But she had seen nothing of Carl. Nor had she seen Pansy, or Robert, or Mrs Latimer. But she could not think about them now. All she could think about was Carl.

So absorbed was she that she did not at first hear the kind words spoken softly next to her.

'My dear. You look frozen. Come with me. My name is Mrs Frampton, and I have a stateroom on board ship. You are welcome to stay there. My maid will draw you a bath, and then you can have something hot to eat before getting in to bed. You must be exhausted.'

With difficulty, Emilia gave her attention to Mrs Frampton.

'No, thank you. That's very kind of you, but I can't leave the rail,' said Emilia. 'I'm watching for someone.'

'A loved one?' asked Dolly with false concern.

'Yes.'

'Your husband?' queried Dolly.

'No, he's not my husband,' said Emilia.

'Your fiancé, then?'

Emilia was too tired to argue.

'I understand your feelings, but if you stay here you will do yourself harm. It's cold, and you are shivering. Will you not let my maid watch for your loved one in your stead? What is his name?'

'Latimer. Mr Carl Latimer.'

'Mary, you are to stand here and check the names of every gentleman who boards the ship. In addition, you must ask each and every survivor if they know what happened to Mr Carl Latimer,' she said to her maid, who had joined them on deck.

'Yes, madam,' said Mary respectfully.

'Come, my dear. You won't be any use to your fiancé if you are exhausted when he arrives. He might need looking after when he gets on board, you know, and you must be rested in order to manage it.'

Worn out by a lack of sleep, by the cold, and by the terrible ordeal she had been through, Emilia agreed. She leant against Dolly as she led her to her stateroom.

'Your clothes are soaking,' Dolly said. 'You must have a warm bath, and then we will see about getting you something to eat before putting you to bed.'

'Well, that's settled,' said Mrs Gisborne to her husband, as she returned to the Braithwaites' stateroom. Mr Gisborne, like his wife, was virtually unmarked by his ordeal. He did not suffer from his wife's complete insensitivity, but he was not a man to worry about things he could do nothing about, and

although he had felt for the souls who had gone down with
Titanic, he had not been overcome. 'At least Miss Cavendish
will be no more threat.'

'You mean she's drowned?' asked Mr Gisborne, looking
up from his paper.

'No. Unfortunately not,' said Mrs Gisborne, putting her hat
down on an elegant table. 'She survived.'

'That's a bit harsh, even for you,' he said uncomfortably.

'Don't be ridiculous,' she sighed, patting her hair and then
sitting down opposite him. 'If she had drowned, it would have
saved us a great many problems. Carl would have returned
to America, grieved for a few weeks, put it behind him and
got on with his life. In other words, he would have married
Isabelle. But now that Miss Cavendish is alive, the future is
by no means so certain, which is why I asked Dolly to take
her to her stateroom. Carl will not be able to find her, and he
will not know she is alive. Nor, if we are careful, will she be
able to find him. They will both assume the other one drowned
and Isabelle might marry Carl yet.'

'The poor girl,' commented Mr Gisborne.

She raised her eyebrows. 'I sometimes wonder about you,
Thomas. Why should Emilia Cavendish be a poor girl, any
more than anyone else? We've all been through a disaster.'

'But we're not all being kept from our loved ones,' he said
gruffly. 'Nor are we being fooled into thinking they're dead.'

She gave an exclamation of impatience. 'It had to be done.
Unless you would like to have Susan and Isabelle living with
us? Because that's what it will come to if Isabelle doesn't
manage to catch Carl Latimer. My sister can't keep up appearances for much longer. Paul left her heavily in debt when he
died, and it has taken all her ingenuity to pretend otherwise.
If anyone guesses what dire straits she is in, it will be impossible for Isabelle to make a suitable match, let alone a good
one. And Isabelle must make a good match. It's the only thing
that can prevent both her and Susan from becoming destitute.
I need hardly remind you that if they become destitute they
will be looking for relatives to take them in. And you know
how you have always disliked Susan.'

His face fell. 'She's a terrible woman,' he said.

'Which is why we must do everything in our power to make sure Isabelle catches Carl,' said Mrs Gisborne with a satisfied air.

'I suppose so,' he said.

She turned her thoughts back to the problem in hand. 'Now, if we can only keep them apart when we land in New York we will have managed the business very well. It shouldn't be too difficult. If we can find out when the Donaldsons mean to disembark, and arrange to be well away from them when they do so, we should be able to manage it. Dolly is going to lend Emilia some clothes in an effort to disguise her appearance. Once she is dressed in a long coat, with a large hat to hide that golden hair, we should be able to make sure Carl won't recognize her, even if he spots her from a distance.'

'And if they meet face to face?' he asked.

'Really, Thomas, why must you be so tiresome? There are over six hundred survivors on board. It's very unlikely that the two of them will meet face to face. We will just have to hope it doesn't happen.'

'You've still got to get him to propose to Isabelle, once he returns to New York,' said Mr Gisborne judiciously.

She agreed. 'That shouldn't prove too difficult either. As long as Isabelle is waiting for him by the pier, which of course she will be, because I telegraphed Susan from the *Titanic* to make sure that that would be the case, she will soon manage to fix him. There's nothing like a few words of kindness after a shock. All she has to do is hold his hand and murmur sympathetic nothings in his ear, and I shouldn't be surprised if they're engaged before the end of the month. A quick wedding would be best, I think – June's a lovely month – and the thing will be done.'

'I just hope it works out the way you've planned it,' said Mr Gisborne, returning to his newspaper.

'Oh, it will,' she said determinedly. 'I'll make sure of it.'

Twelve

E milia scarcely noticed the bath she took or the food she ate before falling into a feverish sleep. She had been soaked through whilst still on *Titanic*, and when she had finally escaped on one of the boats the icy water in the bottom had numbed her feet and legs. The soaking, the exposure, the exertion and the fear had taken their toll, and she collapsed as soon as she was helped into bed.

At last she began to emerge from her slumber. She woke slowly. As she did so, she found herself aching in every bone and muscle. For a moment she could not remember where she was, nor why she should be aching. Her shoulders were painful, and her arms felt as though they were made out of lead. Her hands were sore, and her legs were no better.

Even worse, the stateroom was strange to her. The drapes around the bed were blue, when she remembered very well that they should be gold. She turned her head. She could see the dressing table, but none of her familiar possessions were in view. And then it started to come back to her.

She shut her eyes, trying to block out the memories of *Titanic*'s sinking. She would rather not wake, if waking meant reliving the nightmare. But then she thought of Carl, and her spirit stirred. She must get up. Find him.

'Madam,' she heard a voice calling just outside the room as she sat up. 'Madam, she's awake.'

Mrs Frampton hurried into the bedroom, just as Emilia threw back the covers and tried to get out of bed. As she swung her legs over the side she was overtaken by a wave of dizziness.

'Lie back,' said Mrs Frampton, gently lifting her legs and

166

putting them back on the mattress. 'You have been ill. You must give yourself time to recover.'

Emilia railed at her own weakness, but she had no choice but to do as Mrs Frampton said. Even so, she could not be still. She had to know about Carl.

'Carl,' she said. 'Did you find him? Has he been brought on board?'

She could tell by Mrs Frampton's face that the news was not good.

'I'm sorry, my dear,' said Mrs Frampton, sitting down beside the bed. 'My maid waited by the rail until the last boat was taken on board, but there was no sign of him. I'm very sorry to have to tell you this, but he is not on *Carpathia*.'

'The last boat has been brought on board?' said Emilia in surprise. 'I thought I just dozed off. How long have I slept?'

'It is ten o'clock, my dear—'

'Ten o'clock! Then I've been asleep for almost two hours!'

Mrs Frampton hesitated. Emilia was about to ask her what was the matter, when she noticed that the stateroom curtains were drawn.

'It is ten o'clock in the morning, isn't it?' she asked. 'Or is it ten o'clock in the evening?'

'It is ten o'clock in the evening,' said Dolly. She paused. 'Wednesday evening.'

'Wednesday?' asked Emilia in shock.

The sudden realization that she had slept almost three days away caused her head to throb, and she put her hand to it in an effort to soothe it. If she had slept so long, she must have been ill. And she was still ill, she was forced to admit, as her head throbbed relentlessly. Her attempt to get up had exhausted her, and she had not even managed to swing her legs out of bed. Still, she could not give up.

'I must find Carl,' she said. 'He might have been brought on board before I arrived. Then Mary would not have seen him.'

Mrs Frampton spoke sympathetically. 'I'm sorry my dear, but I thought of that, and sent Mary to check the list of survivors. When she could not find the name of Carl Latimer,

I went to check it myself. It is not that she is not careful, but I wanted to be sure. His name was not on the list.'

'No.' Emilia could not believe it. Carl had gone. She felt a flood of hopelessness wash over her.

'It must be a terrible blow, especially in your weak state, but you will feel better when we reach New York. You will be among friends there. They will help you recover from your loss. You don't think so now, but time is a great healer, and in time your pain will pass,' Mrs Frampton said.

Emilia did not reply. She did not have the energy to speak.

'Rest now. We will reach New York tomorrow. Your friends will be meeting you on the pier when we dock?' she asked.

Emilia nodded. 'Yes. They are going to meet me . . . or they were, but with the ship now arriving on a different day, I'm not sure.'

'Never mind. I will see you safely off the ship and wait with you until I know you are in safe hands. If by any chance your friends do not come to meet you, you will be my guest until such time as you can contact them. Don't worry, my dear, everything will work out in the end, you'll see.'

Emilia was too exhausted to do or say more. She closed her eyes and drifted into welcome oblivion.

In the Donaldsons' stateroom, Mrs Latimer was sitting by Carl's bed, encouraging him to take a drink of tea. She was grieved by the change in him. The vigorous man of a few days before was gone, to be replaced by a thin man with a drawn face. His skin had lost its healthy tone, and was pallid. His eyes had lost their animation, and there were dark rings underneath them. His lips looked bloodless. But he was alive, and for that she was grateful.

She had been so worried in the lifeboat, when she had realized that *Titanic* was going to sink. She had had no idea where Carl was. She had not known if he had managed to get into one of the other boats, or if he was still on the ship.

Pansy had been wonderful. She had worked hard to keep her spirits up, saying she was sure that both Carl and Emilia would be in one of the other boats, but even so it had been an anxious time.

She could still remember the moment she had been brought aboard *Carpathia* on a bosun's chair, and the first thing she had seen had been Carl, stretched out on the deck. He had just been lifted out of another lifeboat, where he had lain on the bottom in the freezing cold and soaking wet for several hours after being pulled out of the water. His skin had been blue. She had thought at first he was dead, but the ship's physician had pronounced him to be alive and she had felt a huge wave of relief. Then Mr Donaldson had come on deck. He had kindly insisted on her having his stateroom, and she had gratefully accepted, following Carl as the stewards had carried him below so that she could put him to bed.

And there he had lain, more dead than alive, whilst she had tended him, with Pansy helping her. Pansy had been wonderful. She had stayed by Carl's bedside each night so that Mrs Latimer could sleep, and had been a great source of comfort and consolation.

Gradually, Carl had started to show signs of life, and she was now trying to get him to take as much sustenance as she could.

'You've got to have something,' she told him. 'The ship's physician said you had to drink as much as possible. Try, please?'

'I can't,' said Carl weakly. 'Not until I know what's happened to Emilia. Are you sure she's not on board? She should be. I saw her get into a lifeboat myself.'

His voice was a shadow of its former rich baritone. But he was as well as could be expected after spending so much time in the freezing waters of the Atlantic.

'Pansy and Robert have been asking everyone on board,' she said gently. 'They've looked all over. No one's seen her, and her name isn't on the survivors' list. I'm sorry, Carl.'

'One of the other ships could have picked her up,' he said. 'I heard Captain Smith speaking to the first officer. There were a number of ships on their way. The *Baltic*, the *Olympic* – any one of them could have taken her on board.'

None of the other ships answering *Titanic*'s distress call had rescued any survivors, but the fiction allowed Carl to hope, and hope was important to him if he was to regain his strength. So she said nothing.

'I must find out when the other ships will be docking in New York,' he said. 'Then I can be there to meet them.'

'Well, I'll ask Captain Rostron when they're going to get there,' said Mrs Latimer. 'Now, drink your tea.'

Reluctantly he took a sip, then another, and thanks to his mother's coaxing he slowly drank the whole cup.

'It makes a change to have you looking after me,' he said with a weak smile.

'I should think so too. When I think of how I stayed in bed all day, well, I can't believe it. We'll have you up in no time, as long as you do as I tell you,' she said.

He smiled, but his thoughts could not be diverted for long. 'How long is it until *Carpathia* reaches New York?' he asked.

'Not long. We've had a lot of bad weather since *Titanic* sank. It's making it hard for the crew to know when we'll get there, but it ought to be some time tomorrow.'

'The sooner we arrive in New York the better,' he said. His eyes wandered round the bedroom. 'It was good of Donaldson to give us his stateroom.'

'Everyone's been very kind,' she said. 'The passengers and crew couldn't have been kinder. They've all done everything they can to make us feel better. Pansy and Robert said the same thing this morning. Nothing's been too much trouble for them.'

He closed his eyes,

'You're tired,' she said. 'You'd better get some rest.'

Looking at him, she realized he had not heard her. He had already fallen asleep. She stroked his hair back from his face. It pained her to see him looking so ill. But in time he would recover.

She left him sleeping and went through into the sitting room. She had not been there long when there was a knock on the door.

Pansy, she thought.

Pansy had been such a comfort to her through the last few days. She really didn't know how she would have managed without her. She had had Miss Epson to help her, of course, but her companion was not of a practical turn of mind and tended to become agitated at the slightest thing. Mrs Latimer had gratefully accepted Pansy's help to watch over Carl, and they had nursed him back to health together.

She opened the door.

Pansy was looking thinner than she had done a few days before, and her expression was more sombre. Her spirits had been affected by the ordeal, and although she was still of a positive turn of mind, her light-hearted gaiety had disappeared.

'Well, I'm glad to see you. It's kind of you to help out like this, and don't think I don't know it,' said Mrs Latimer, as she invited Pansy in.

'I'm only too happy to do it,' said Pansy.

The two ladies sat down. Both were dressed strangely. They had escaped from *Titanic* with only the clothes they had been wearing when the ship had gone down, and those clothes had been ruined by salt water. Female passengers on board *Carpathia* had kindly donated clothes to all the survivors of *Titanic*, and both Pansy and Mrs Latimer were now wearing clothes which were oddly mismatched. Pansy's skirt was too small, and she had not been able to fasten it properly round the waist. Her blouse was too big, and she had had to turn the sleeves over at the cuff to prevent them falling over her hands. Mrs Latimer was wearing a dress which hung from her like a sack, and which was far too long. Still, they had the advantage of being clean, warm and dry.

'How is he?' asked Pansy.

'A bit better,' said Mrs Latimer. 'He went to sleep again this afternoon, and he's had some tea. But he's still poorly.'

'And does he know yet?' asked Pansy.

Mrs Latimer shook her head. 'No. He thinks she'll have been picked up by one of the other ships, and he's hoping she's still alive. I can't tell him, at least not yet.'

'Perhaps it's better that way,' said Pansy. 'At least he will be rested before he has to bear the shock of discovering that none of the other ships have any survivors on board. I still can't believe that Emilia is gone. I've asked everyone on the ship if they've seen her, and checked the list of survivors three times, but there is no trace of her.'

'She was so full of life,' said Mrs Latimer with a sigh. 'If only she'd got into the boat with us, right at the beginning, she'd have missed the worst of things, like we did. I know it was cold in the lifeboats, and the sight of the ship sinking – well, it's best not to think of that. But we're both still here.'

They fell silent.

It seemed so peaceful in the sitting room that it was almost impossible to believe what had happened just a few short days before. The curtains were pulled cosily across the portholes. The clock ticked complacently on the mantelpiece, and the electric lights bathed the rose-upholstered furniture in a warm glow.

'That wretched man!' burst out Pansy suddenly. 'He has a lot to answer for.'

'Barker,' nodded Mrs Latimer. 'He paid for it, though.'

Pansy looked at her enquiringly.

'Carl told me the rest of it when you'd gone to lie down. You know it was Barker who took her, just before she got into the boat, and you know Carl managed to find her again, but you don't know that Barker got his comeuppance. He tried to get on one of the lifeboats dressed as a woman. Emilia pulled his hat off. One of the officers hit him with the butt of his gun, and Barker toppled over the side of the ship. He wasn't wearing a life jacket.'

'I should not be pleased,' said Pansy, 'but I am.' She fell silent again, thinking. 'But Emilia . . . I still can't understand it. Carl said he saw her get into the boat.'

Mrs Latimer stood up and went over to one of the lamps on a console table. She switched it on, adding another pool of light to the room.

'Well, yes, but Carl was knocked away by a wave. With the ship sinking fast and the water rising, she could have been washed out of it. And then, what with all the suction as the ship went down . . .'

The two women fell silent.

'What will you do?' asked Pansy at last.

'Go back to New York and look after Carl.'

'Do you think he will go on as before when we return to New York?'

'I'd like to think so, but I just don't know. I used to think he'd get married, find a nice girl and settle down, but I'm not sure now.'

'There will be plenty of young ladies willing to tempt him,' said Pansy.

'Oh, yes, there'll be plenty to try, but I don't think they'll do it. They're pretty girls but they're cold. Emilia was warm. She made Carl a different man, like he used to be, before he got making all this money. Not that I'm saying it hasn't been useful, but there's other things in life.' She sighed. 'Well, I'll worry about that another day. Right now, I just want to get back home.'

Pansy looked at her sympathetically. Once back in New York, Mrs Latimer would have to face the ordeal of telling Carl that the other ships had not taken aboard any survivors.

Pansy did not envy her the task.

Emilia stood patiently in the sitting room, waiting for Mrs Frampton's maid to finish her packing. She was wearing some clothes kindly lent to her by Mrs Frampton. They were too large, and intended for a woman who was twice her age, but still, she was grateful for them. She was wearing a long coat down to her ankles, a stole around her shoulders, and a large-brimmed hat on her head. Mrs Frampton had taken care to muffle her up, telling her that the weather was cold and foggy. Still weakened by her ordeal, she was even more weakened by the knowledge that Carl had not survived. But she was determined not to let the depths of her feelings show. Mrs Frampton had been very kind to her, and Emilia did not want to burden her benefactress with a display of grief.

'Is everything ready?' asked Mrs Frampton as she cast her eye over her luggage, neatly packed and stacked by the door of the stateroom.

'Yes, madam,' said Mary.

'Good.' Mrs Frampton tuned to Emilia. 'The ship will be docking any minute. It's time for us to go ashore.'

Emilia should have been looking forward to it. With Barker gone, and Charlie and Julia waiting for her, it held the promise of an interesting holiday in New York. But the joy had gone out of her. Since learning that Carl had not been rescued, she had lost her interest in life.

'Come, my dear, take my arm.'

Together she and Emilia made their way through the ship to the gangplank.

'Stay with me, my dear,' said Mrs Frampton. 'If your friends have not come to meet you, you will come home with me as arranged. I will be happy to look after you until you can send them word of where you are staying.'

'Thank you. You're very kind,' said Emilia.

'Don't mention it. It's the least I can do after all you've endured,' said Mrs Frampton with false sympathy.

There was the sound of rain pattering on the covered roof of the dock as they left the ship. Lightning flashed intermittently.

'It's a good thing the weather wasn't like this on the night *Titanic* sank, or no one would have been saved,' said Mrs Frampton. 'The weather has been stormy ever since that fateful night.'

'Yes, madam,' said Mary.

It was true. Emilia knew that if a storm had raged, no one would have been saved. Launching the lifeboats would have been difficult enough, and surviving on a turbulent sea would have been impossible. She should be grateful she had her own life. But with Carl gone, it was hard for her to be grateful about anything.

As she set foot on the gangplank she looked down at the pier. Ranged around it were friends and relatives of those who had survived the disaster, looking up at the ship with anxious faces. White-clad ambulance surgeons stood in a group nearby, in case they should be needed. Sisters of Mercy were on hand in their black clothes, and there were a number of priests.

Light bulbs flashed as photographers took pictures for the newspapers. Reporters stood next to them with notebooks and pencils.

Emilia found it daunting. Her nerves had still not fully recovered from the ordeal, and she was apprehensive about leaving the pier. To her relief, however, the police had a strong presence. They were holding the crowds back and keeping the situation under control.

She paused halfway down the gangplank, searching the crowds for a sight of Charlie. Her eyes roamed over all the strange faces. Then she felt herself relax as she saw him. There was no mistaking his round face, black hair, and round body, even beneath a long raincoat and bowler hat. Next to him was a dark-haired woman with a good-natured countenance and a heart-shaped face. She was wearing a fashionably-cut coat and a large hat. She must be Julia.

Kind though Mrs Frampton had been, it was an enormous relief for Emilia to see them.

'There are my friends,' said Emilia, turning to Mrs Frampton.

'I'm so pleased,' said Mrs Frampton. 'It makes such a difference to have loved ones looking after you at a time like this. Go to them, my dear.'

'Thank you for everything you have done for me. It was very kind of you to take me in, and look after me when I was ill.'

'It was nothing,' said Mrs Frampton with a wide smile. 'Don't mention it.'

Emilia hurried down the gang plank and across the dock.

Charlie pushed his way through the crowd. A policeman tried to bar his way, but after a brief discussion he was allowed to pass. He met Emilia halfway across the dock.

'Emilia!' he said. 'We have been so worried about you. Ever since *Titanic* sank, Julia and I have been on tenterhooks, wondering whether you would be alive or dead. It is so good to see you, especially in one piece. You must have had a terrible time, but it's over now. Julia and I mean to look after you. How are you feeling?' he went on, as he guided her through the crowd to Julia.

'A little pulled down,' she said.

She made light of her troubles, not wanting to upset him any more than necessary. It would not be fair to burden Charlie and Julia with her grief. Besides, she did not want to talk about it. They knew nothing about Carl, and her feelings were too raw to allow her to speak of him. The ordeal she had suffered aboard *Titanic* was enough to explain her low spirits, and they would not look for anything further.

She and Charlie reached the young woman Emilia had seen from the gangplank.

'This is Julia,' said Charlie.

There was no mistaking the note of pride in his voice. It was easy to see why. Julia was a beautiful young woman with gleaming dark hair and smiling eyes. Her clothes were well cut, her knee-length coat being fastened round the middle with a wide buckled belt, and her wrap-over skirt tapering towards her neat ankles. A wide-brimmed hat decorated with a single feather completed her outfit. Charlie was evidently in love with her, and as Julia looked up at him, Emilia could see his feelings were returned.

'I'm pleased to meet you,' said Emilia.

'And I'm so pleased to meet you,' said Julia, taking her hand. 'It's such a relief to know that you're safe. When we heard about the *Titanic* we feared the worst. I cannot tell you what Charlie went through when he thought you might have been drowned. It is such a relief to us to have you here with us. Now everything will be all right.'

'I tried to send you a telegraph to let you know I had survived,' said Emilia, as Charlie led them to his waiting motor car. 'A kindly woman, a Mrs Frampton, took me in and looked after me in her stateroom. She instructed her maid to send you a telegraph, but the telegraph office was kept busy with official communications and I doubt if it was ever sent.'

'That doesn't matter now,' said Charlie, pushing aside a reporter who was waving his notebook under Emilia's nose, and guiding her past the ambulances drawn up beside the pier, whilst all around them the crowd surged forward as survivors tried to find their families. 'All that matters is that you are safe.'

'I'll be glad when we reach the car,' said Julia, as she was jostled by the crowd.

'Not much further now,' said Charlie.

Before long they reached the motor car. Charlie opened the doors for Emilia and Julia, then closed them again when they had stepped inside. He himself climbed into the driver's seat.

Once inside the car, with the doors closed, the noise of the dock receded. Charlie switched on the engine then they pulled away. As they left the dock behind them, Emilia felt some of the horror of her ordeal recede with it. But she was left with an aching pain.

'We're so sorry you had to go through such a terrible ordeal,' said Julia. 'But now that you are with us you must stay for as long as you like. We will soon have you on your feet again, won't we, Charlie?'

'Of course we will,' Charlie said with a reassuring smile.

Their kindness was balm to Emilia's troubled spirit. Even so, although she tried to put a good face on things she could not hide her hurt.

'Don't worry, you will soon feel as right as rain,' said Julia, sensing her low mood and giving her hand a squeeze. 'It's not as though you lost a loved one. You don't think so now, but you'll soon recover, you'll see.'

Julia's words, kindly meant, awoke all Emilia's grief, and as she stepped out of the car when they reached Charlie's apartment, her tears mingled with the rain.

Carl stood in his office next to a huge window and looked out over the city. His office was on the top floor of the building, and from his high vantage point he could see the life of New York teeming below him. But the one life he wanted to see was not there. He had tried to keep his mind on his work, but it had been to no avail. The window always drew him. He could not concentrate on anything since his return to New York. He could think of only one thing: Emilia.

Not that he had let it show. He had kept up appearances,

attending to his business and going to the functions he'd agreed to attend before leaving for Europe, but his heart was not in it.

He had much to be thankful for. He knew that. His mother had been saved, as had Pansy, Robert and Hutton. He himself had survived, but he had lost Emilia. His mind went back to the beautiful young woman who had claimed his heart. She had been nothing like the society ladies he had met, who were artificial in word and deed, with their every gesture calculated and practised to the highest degree. Nor had she been like the women he had known in his youth; ground down by work and poverty and yet still good-hearted and earthy. She had been an alluring mixture of both worlds: delicate and beautiful, but with a naturalness and honesty about her that he had found irresistible. Time and again, his thoughts returned to her, and to the feelings and experiences they had shared aboard *Titanic*. It had been the most stimulating and enriching time of his life. But it had been too brief.

His thoughts moved on, to the moment he had put her into the lifeboat. He had gone into the sea with the satisfaction of thinking she would be safe. Discovering that she had not been rescued had been terrible, but he had still clung on to hope. One of the other rescue ships, arriving on the scene shortly after *Carpathia*, could have taken her on board. It was with this hope in mind that he had arrived in New York.

And there to meet him on the pier had been, not Emilia, but Miss Stott. It could not have been worse. Miss Stott, with her shallowness and her hypocrisy, was the complete opposite of Emilia's honesty and warmth. Her condolences had disgusted him, and he had been brusque, even rude. He had made it clear that he had no intention of marrying her, and had all but physically pushed past her in his hurry to find out if any of the other rescue ships had taken Emilia on board. The pain of discovering that none of them had taken any survivors out of the sea had been intense. But even the pain had been preferable to the numbness that had gripped him ever since. He had tried to throw himself into his work, without success. He could think about one thing and one thing only: that he had lost her.

Charlie and Julia welcomed Emilia into their lives and their home. They took her shopping, replacing the clothes she had lost when *Titanic* sank, and endeavoured to lift her spirits by involving her in small gatherings of their friends. In return, Emilia made an effort to be an ideal guest. She showed an interest in the sights of New York, although really she would much rather have stayed in the apartment, and exclaimed over the shops, although the idea of shopping had never been so unappetising. She talked politely to their friends, smiling at their jokes, but all the time she was aching inside. Her greatest wish was to be in Ireland. She was looking forward to retiring to the quiet village in which her godmother lived, where she would be able to unburden herself, sharing her ordeal and her pain at losing Carl, and in time, perhaps, finding balm for her spirit.

Her godmother's letter was a great comfort. She was reading it for the third time as she sat on the window seat in Charlie's apartment, looking forward to the day when she would be able to speak to her godmother in person.

I was so relieved when I received your telegraph to say that you were all right, Emilia. We heard about the disaster, and were terribly worried but now we know you're safe we can breathe again. It was lucky you met Charlie in New York. It must make things much pleasanter for you to have a friend to stay with. We can't wait to have you here. Do you know yet when you will be arriving? I do hope you're not afraid to make the journey. Disasters like the one you endured happen very infrequently, and it is very unlikely that anything will happen on your next voyage. I know this is easy for me to say. I was not on board *Titanic*, and I am not facing a sea journey, but even so I hope it will not be too long before I see you again.

It would not be long, Emilia thought. She had already booked her passage. In less than a week she would be sailing to Ireland.

She folded the letter, then let her gaze wander out of the window. It was a fine day in early May, with a blue sky and a glimmer of sunshine. Everything was burgeoning into new life. Spring flowers filled the park, and pink and white blossoms covered the trees. Children were playing, running about under the watchful eyes of their nursemaids. But even that pleasant scene could not dispel the blackness that had clung to her since Carl had been lost.

Still, she was pleased for Charlie and Julia. They were to attend a garden party that day and the fine weather would make it very pleasant for them. She, too, was to go, and although she was not looking forward to it, she had the consolation of knowing that it was the last engagement she would have to attend before she sailed for Ireland.

She folded up her letter. It was time for her to dress. Julia would soon be arriving, and then the three of them would go to the Malcasters. She went through into her bedroom and put on one of the dresses Charlie had kindly bought her. It was an understated Empire-line gown in shades of soft blue, and the colour suited her, but she scarcely noticed it. Ever since losing Carl the joy had gone out of her, and she hardly saw what she wore.

She heard Julia arriving. Putting on her wide-brimmed hat and gloves, she went into the hall. There was Julia, dressed in a beautiful flame-coloured peg-top dress, and Charlie, smart in a lounge suit.

'I'm so looking forward to this,' said Julia, as they went out to the car. 'The Malcasters have the most beautiful home, and the gardens are superb. You will love them, Emilia. Won't she, Charlie?'

'Of course she will,' said Charlie heartily, as they climbed into the car and set off. 'What could be better on a summer's day than going to a garden party? It'll put a little colour in your cheeks, Emilia. You're looking too pasty. We don't want your godmother to think we've been mistreating you when you go to Ireland.'

Emilia smiled at his pleasantry, and said she could not have been better treated.

They were soon at the Malcasters. When they arrived, Emilia could see why Julia and Charlie had been looking forward to the afternoon. The Malcasters' house was a grand white edifice with sparkling windows and an immaculate sweeping drive, and the gardens surrounding it were magnificent. Even in her low state she could appreciate them. The lawns were emerald, and were so neat their edges appeared to have been cut with a knife. They led away from the house in all directions, being flanked with a lake at one side and a high hedge at the other. In front of the hedge were expansive flower beds, where plants had been arranged with an artist's eye. Cool blues and whites were enlivened with touches of yellow, and textures contrasted attractively with each other. A path led through the hedge, and Emilia caught glimpses of hot coloured flowers, reds, oranges and pinks beyond. Her eye returned to the lawn, where tables covered with white cloths were laid out and where waiters walked round with trays of champagne.

Emilia, Charlie and Julia were greeted by the Malcasters, a young couple who had bought a houseful of antiques from Charlie on their marriage. Mr Malcaster was a stocky man, with dark hair and brown eyes, whilst his wife was an ethereal beauty with blonde hair and green eyes. They were both keenly interested in England, and were delighted to meet Emilia. Mr Malcaster's grandfather had been English, and he and his wife were keen to learn as much as they could about the country. They talked to Emilia at length, asking her about Southampton, and eliciting from her details of everything down to the kind of weather England had been having when she had left. Tactfully, they avoided all mention of *Titanic*. Emilia was grateful. She did not think she could have talked about it with equanimity.

They finally turned their attention to their other guests, and Charlie introduced Emilia to a number of other people who were his friends. She joined in with the conversation, making an effort to seem as though she was enjoying herself, but in reality she found the afternoon something of a strain, and the only thing that could console her was the knowledge that, after today, she would not have to make such an effort again. After half an hour of doing her duty, however, she could take it no longer, and she slipped away, saying she was going to find another glass of champagne.

She went across the lawns. Beyond the hedge, she hoped she might be able to find some quiet. She took the path that led through it, and discovered that on the other side of the hedge it veered to the left before leading through a shrubbery. It looked secluded in the shrubbery, and she followed the path as it snaked through the large bushes so that before long, when she turned round, she could not see the rest of the gardens. She was completely cut off, and gave a sigh of relief to know that she would not be introduced to any new people, or have to make polite conversation or laugh at anyone's jokes.

At length the path emerged in a circular clearing. Round the edges were three stone seats, where she would be able to rest for a little while before returning to the party. She was about to take a seat when she felt a presence behind her. The hairs stood up on her arms, and the air seemed to be filled with an electric charge. She stopped breathing. There was only one person who could make her feel like that. Carl.

But Carl was dead.

'Hello, Emilia.'

The voice was so husky it made her mouth grow dry, and so familiar it made her heart turn over in her chest.

Was it possible? Could it be him?

But no, he had drowned.

What then? A ghost? Were there ghosts? Did they exist? Could they return to speak to the living, if they had something still to say?

She was longing to turn round, but did not dare. If she turned round and saw nothing she would have to face up to the fact that the voice had been a product of her imagination, a hallucination, a memory carried on the breeze. If she stayed where she was she could pretend, just for a minute, that it belonged to Carl.

'Won't you speak to me?'

It came again.

Was she mad? Was she hearing things? Was she longing to find him so badly that her mind was giving him to her? Or had he, by some miracle, survived?

'Carl?'

Her voice came out as a whisper. She hardly dare say his name; hardly dare turn; hardly dare hope it was him. But at last she had to know.

Summoning all her courage she slowly turned, wanting to know the truth and yet fearing it at the same time. She saw the edge of his jacket; the side of his face; and then she saw the whole of him. He was altered. His lounge suit hung from him. There were dark rings under his eyes. His cheekbones were more pronounced. But he was still Carl. And he was alive.

She didn't quite dare believe it.

'Carl?' she breathed.

He smiled, and it lit his eyes. They were the same eyes that had roved over her on the ship, that had drunk her in; the eyes that had looked into her own so deeply when he had put her into the lifeboat.

She took a step towards him, hesitantly at first, then he opened his arms and she ran into them. He caught her fast and held her close.

'You're alive!' she said wonderingly, pulling away a little when at last he let her go.

'Yes, my love. And so are you.'

He took her hands and looked her up and down as if he still could not believe she was real.

'But what are you doing here? How did you survive?' she gasped.

He put his arm round her and led her to one of the seats. He sat down, and she sat next to him, leaning against him, still not able to believe he was real. She put her hand on his arm and stroked her thumb across it. She felt the hardness of his muscle beneath the fabric of his coat, but even then she was not convinced.

She felt him drop kisses on the top of her head and gave a deep sigh. It was so wonderful, it couldn't be true.

'I was about to get into the boat with you when I was washed off the deck,' he began.

'I remember,' she said, her voice hollow. It had been a terrible moment.

He held her closer.

'There was no way I could get back into the boat,' he explained. 'I knew my only chance of survival was to swim away from the ship in order to avoid the suction and then hope I could find some wreckage to cling to, or a half empty lifeboat to climb into. I kicked away from the ship with all my might. Once away from the ship I saw an upturned lifeboat. It was one of the collapsible boats the crew didn't mange to launch in time. I swam towards it, but there were already so many men standing on it that if I had climbed aboard, it would have been swamped. I swam on. The cold was intense, and it wasn't long before I was numb. I drifted in and out of consciousness. At last, I saw a lifeboat nearby. I struck out for it and was pulled on board. I lay in the bottom of the boat, scarcely knowing whether I was alive or dead. I remember very little after that, until I found myself on board *Carpathia* in the Donaldsons' stateroom. My mother was there, tending me. I asked for you, but she told me she didn't know where you were. I begged her to find you. She wouldn't leave me, but she sent Pansy to look for you.'

'Pansy and your mother were saved as well?' she asked.

'Yes.'

She laid her head on his shoulder, and as she did so the sun came out from behind a cloud. It seemed like years since she had felt it. After the cold and dark of the last few weeks, it was a joyous feeling.

'It's a dream,' she sighed. 'I know it is. But it's such a good dream I don't want to wake up. Go on.'

'They could not find you,' he said, kissing her hair again. 'I comforted myself with the thought that more than one ship had been hailed when *Titanic* was sinking, and I was adamant that one of them must have taken you on board. My mother knew it wasn't the case, but she didn't want me to know the truth until I was well enough to face it. As soon as we returned to New York I found out you had not been rescued. I had lost you.'

He pulled her even closer, wrapping his arms more tightly around her as though he would never let her go.

'But you are here,' he said. 'And I still don't know how it is possible. Pansy looked all over the ship for you. She checked the list of survivors and your name was not there. Once we returned to New York, I checked the list myself. '

'I don't know how you came to overlook it,' said Emilia, 'but it was there. I, too, was taken into a stateroom. I was standing by the rail of the *Carpathia* watching every boat that came. Despite my exhaustion, I refused all attempts of the crew to make me go below and have a hot meal. I was sure you were alive, and I had to find you. And then one of *Carpathia*'s passengers, a very kind and generous lady, saw me, and coaxed me to leave my place. Her maid would watch in my stead, she said. I was so exhausted by that time I could barely stand. She took me to her stateroom and looked after me. I was ill with cold and fear, and suffering the effects of exposure. Once I had recovered a little, I wanted to search for you, but I was too weak to get out of bed. She sent her maid to check the list of survivors. You were not on it.'

'But I *was* on it,' he said, puzzled.

'No.' She shook her head. 'Neither you, nor your mother, nor Pansy or Robert, were on the list of survivors. Mrs Frampton checked the list herself.'

'Frampton?' he asked. He put her gently away from him so that he could look at her. 'This Mrs Frampton,' he asked. 'Was she a tall, graceful woman with red hair?'

Emilia was surprised at his question. 'Yes. Do you know her?'

His mouth set in a straight line. 'She is a friend of Mrs Gisborne's.'

'I don't see ...' Realization began to dawn. 'You don't mean that she took me in deliberately, so that she could lead me to believe you were dead?' she asked in horror.

He nodded. 'And so that she could give a false name to the officers when they asked about you for the list of survivors.

That way, I would not know you were alive. And by telling you that my name was not on the list, she was able to prevent you finding out that I had been saved.'

'The wickedness of it,' whispered Emilia in horror. 'And all so that you would marry Isabelle?'

'When I think of the harm that woman nearly caused . . .' he said, his eyes turbulent and his lips white.

'But she didn't,' said Emilia, lifting her hand to caress his cheek.

He turned to look at her and his eyes warmed. 'No. You're right.' He caught her hand and kissed it, then turned it over and kissed the palm. 'She didn't. Emilia, I love you. Against all hope I've found you. Will you do me the very great honour of becoming my wife?'

She turned up her face to his. 'Yes, I will,' she said.

He kissed her softly on the lips, and she returned his kiss in full measure. It had never been sweeter. She had found Carl, and she was to be his wife. She had never dreamt such happiness existed.

They stayed there, wrapped up in each other, until the sun began to sink lower in the sky.

'We must return to the other guests,' said Carl at last.

He stood up, drawing her with him. As he did, he saw her smile. He looked at her enquiringly.

'I was just thinking,' she said, with a happy sigh. 'What a lot I will have to tell my godmother.'